Red River Love

LANA STONE

Copyright

Copyright © 2024 by Lana Stone
Loving Hearts Publishing LLC
2880W Oakland Park Blvd
Suite 225C
Oakland Park, FL 33311
If you would like to receive a free novel and be alerted when my next book is published, visit: https://lana-stone.com/. There, like over 9000 fans before you, you can sign up for my newsletter.

Blurb

50 Shades meets Heartland in this funny and steamy Enemies to Lovers novel by international bestselling author Lana Stone.

June Farley: Years ago, I left Merryville in a hurry to protect my broken heart. I drowned my sorrows in work until I became New York's most successful interior designer. Today, I'm back and I'm running into the man I never wanted to see again. John Key. He makes me a job offer I can't refuse. I hate him for seeing through me. I hate him for being irresistible. I hate him for the fact that I still love him. And I hate him for figuring out bit by bit why I'm here.

John Key: Years ago, the love of my life moved to New York and took my heart with her. Today she's back in Texas, but she still has my heart. She acts like she hates me. But I've long since seen behind her façade. She still finds me irresistible. She still loves me. She's mine. I know that for a fact. And I'll make sure she knows it too.

Red River is a spin-off of the popular Billionaires of New York series, which tells the story of the Keys family in Texas. Each book is about a different couple and you shouldn't read this series if you don't want a lot of spice in your chili con carne, because there is more than one use for the lasso and the riding crop on this ranch.

Chapter 1 – June

Wow, even though I'd been gone for years, Merryville hadn't changed a bit. The sun always seemed to shine here. The small pothole right after the rusty town sign was still there, and so was the green-painted motel that stood out from the natural wood-clad houses. Even Dotty's old mail truck, held together by spare parts, was still the same.

Home.

Still, I didn't feel comfortable. Since I'd left for New York years ago, everything had changed, you just couldn't see it.

I actually wanted to take care of what I came for as quickly as possible, but when I saw the red neon tubes of Sue's Diner in the distance, I slowed the car down.

Nobody could pass by the diner without eating a piece of Sue's world-best apple crumble pie. Neither could I, really. Especially not when I hadn't eaten a comparable pie in ages.

A quick stop for the best pie in the world couldn't hurt, right?

In my head, the plan was very simple. Go in, eat, go out. No drama, no heartache, no...

To prove to myself that I was no longer the weak girl from back then, I had to eat a piece of pie now more than ever.

I parked my light green Mini between two huge pickup trucks and got out of the air-conditioned car. It was damn hot, even by Texas standards.

As I opened the door, a buzz of voices and the scent of pie, coffee, and fried bacon wafted towards me. The bell hanging above the entrance announced my visit, and Sue, who was standing at the counter pouring coffee, turned to look at me.

Even she hadn't changed. She wore her yellow dress with a red apron, the uniform of every waitress in the diner. Her gray hair was tied in a bun with a pen stuck in it.

"Hello Sue," I greeted her warmly. Then I sat down in an empty seat right at the counter.

"June? June Farley?" she asked in surprise, peering over the rim of her glasses.

I nodded. "That's right."

"Let me look at you, you're hardly recognizable!"

Sue was right. I had traded my old long jeans for urban designer dresses, and my boots for flats and heels. I had adapted to New York, otherwise I would never have had the chance to become one of the most sought-after interior designers.

"It's been a while since I was last here," I said sheepishly, smoothing out the black fabric of my dress.

"A while? My goodness, it's been ages!" Sue replied in a shrill voice.

"I think it's nice to be back too." On one hand, it was true, I loved my hometown, but on the other hand, I wanted to get out of here as quickly as possible. There were too many impressions reminding me why I had fled to the other end of the country.

Sue leaned forward conspiratorially, poured me some coffee, and whispered, "So? Is anyone in New York giving me competition?"

I laughed out loud.

"No, Sue. Nobody can compete with your pie. Why do you think I'm here?"

"Good answer," Sue said, grinning. Then she portioned two large pieces of her homemade apple crumble pie onto a plate and set it down in front of me. "These are on the house."

"Thank you."

Carefully, I took a small bite and sighed.

Sue's pie was to my soul what water meant to someone dying of thirst. It was perfect, and for a moment, I felt at home again.

"Tell me, what are you doing here?" Sue asked while serving other guests.

"I need to take care of the rest of the Farley Ranch," I sighed.

"Oh," Sue replied. "I'm so sorry it's not a happier occasion bringing you to visit us."

My grandparents had passed away some time ago, and my parents had sold most of our ranch when I was already in New York. But I had to take care of the piece my grandparents had left me myself, as stated in the will.

"It's okay, I still think it's nice to be here," I waved off. I didn't tell Sue that I had struggled with myself for almost half a year to finally travel to Merryville.

The door bell rang once more, and when I saw who entered the diner, I buried my face in my long brown hair.

Rachel Pearson was the second to last person I wanted to encounter here, because she was the reason I had left Merryville in the first place.

She went to the counter without sparing me or any of the other guests a glance.

"A latte macchiato with fat-free milk and cinnamon," Rachel ordered, drumming her artificial fingernails on the wood.

"Coming right up," Sue replied. She turned away from Rachel and rolled her eyes in annoyance, which made me giggle. Rachel looked at me with a frown, then grinned from ear to ear.

"June!" she called out with artificial enthusiasm.

My arch-enemy gave me a fake smile and was just waiting to stab me in the back one more time. Never had I wished more for the ground to open up and swallow me whole.

"Rachel," I replied with less enthusiasm.

"How long have you been here?" Rachel asked.

I shrugged. "Just arrived."

"Oh, then welcome back," Rachel said with a broad smile. We both knew perfectly well that she was one of the reasons why I couldn't stand Merryville any longer.

"Thanks," I replied with a smile, trying not to let my hatred and anger show.

"So how's it going in New York? It must be so exciting to work in that huge city! How's your little business doing?"

I swallowed my frustration. If Rachel had asked me two weeks and a day ago how my little business was doing, I would have answered that it was going great. More than great. I was one of the most sought-after interior designers in the city and booked solid for months. Unfortunately, my partner, an architect with a penchant for risky business strategies, had run our company into the ground. Really hard. Without a seatbelt or airbag.

And now I had to figure out how to get my neck out of the noose that was tightening around it.

"Good," I lied. I neither wanted to rub my failed existence in Rachel's face nor worry Sue, who was following our conversation attentively. "There's a lot to do."

"I hope you're still staying until the summer festival? You surely remember how much time and money my family puts into the event."

"Of course," I said thoughtfully.

Who didn't know that? Rachel's family had more money than all the residents within a fifty-mile radius combined. She was the daughter of none other than Richard Pearson, who made his fortune in oil, while her mother focused on breeding show jumpers.

"So? Can we count on you?" Rachel asked, tilting her head.

"No, probably not. I just need to sort out a few things here and then I'll be gone again."

"That's a shame," Rachel replied, still with a beaming smile. Then she took her latte macchiato with fat-free milk and cinnamon and disappeared as quickly as she had come.

Sue leaned over the counter. "Unlike Rachel, I really do think it's a shame that you're only in Merryville for such a short time. But you must have a lot to do in New York, right?"

I smiled painfully. "Yes."

The thought of New York made me shudder just as much as the thought of Merryville.

"Really too bad. Henry and Katy would have surely wished for you to see your grandchildren grow up in their house someday." Sue winked at me. She had always had a talent for appealing to one's conscience.

I put a twenty-dollar bill on the table and stood up.

"It was nice to see you again," I said goodbye to Sue.

"For me too! And don't you dare disappear without a word again," Sue said with a raised index finger, and I raised my arms in a placating gesture.

"I promise I'll stock up on a month's supply of apple crumble pie before I head back to New York."

And just as I was about to leave Sue's Diner, I encountered the person I least wanted to see again.

The man because of whom I hated Rachel so much.

The person who had broken my heart.

The man because of whom I had left Merryville.

John Key, whose hazel eyes looked directly at me.

Chapter 2 – John

I WIPED THE SWEAT from my forehead with my free hand. On my right shoulder, I balanced a sack of horse feed. Damn, if this heat wave didn't end soon, we'd have a real problem. We hadn't seen a single drop of rain in weeks, and the livestock was slowly running out of pasture grass.

I heaved the heavy feed sack onto the bed of my pickup and grabbed the next one. On Ellis's orders, Sophia had ordered twelve sacks of horse feed. And who had to drive into town, load them up, and unload them later? That's right, me. And why?

Because I was their favorite brother.

Most of the time, I felt flattered when Sophia or Elli called me their favorite brother out of all their siblings - we were five. But the title came with some burdens.

Just before the end of my arduous hauling, my smartphone rang. I threw the last sack onto the truck bed and answered the call.

"What's up, sis?" I asked.

"John? Where are you? Elli and I were about to file a missing person's report with the sheriff," Sophia giggled, but I could hear real concern in her voice.

"I'm still in Merryville, hauling your overpriced mash," I teased Sophia.

"It's not overpriced mash," she snorted. Although I couldn't see her, I knew exactly that she was rolling her eyes while at least three curly strands of hair bounced across her face. "Elli knows exactly what she's doing. So let her do her job."

"Then why am I doing her job?"

Elli was the youngest in our family, but when it came to horses, everyone trusted her advice.

"Because you're our favorite brother," Sophia answered sweetly.

"When does your favorite brother get a trip to the Rocky Mountains? Or a new car? As a token of your appreciation, I mean."

"Because we know you love your work."

Sophia wasn't wrong about that. I loved my life and my work on Red Rivers, our family ranch.

"I'll be back in twenty minutes," I said, closing the tailgate of the truck and leaning against it exhaustedly.

"Alright, drive safely!"

"Always."

Just as I was about to hang up, Rachel Pearson walked towards me. We used to have the same circle of friends, the same hangouts. But for years, we hadn't exchanged more than standard pleasantries. Since that one incident, I avoided Rachel as much as I could. And she avoided me. She strode past me in her high heels, balancing a coffee cup in her hand.

"You know what, Sophia? I'll need a bit longer. I'm going to grab a burger at Sue's."

"Make it two. With extra bacon," said Sophia. I could hear Elli's voice in the background. "And a Manhattan sandwich for Elli."

"Got it."

Sue's Diner was, as always, pretty full, and normally I always saw a few familiar faces - in Merryville, everyone knew everyone through the grapevine - but one particular face made my heart skip a beat.

June Farley. Was it really her?

Was she the woman who had traveled to New York ages ago and taken my damn heart with her?

No doubt, it was her. Her dark brown, long hair that was as soft as velvet, her piercing green eyes that shone brighter than the sun, and her beautiful smile I would recognize among millions. When she saw me through the window, her smile faded.

I wondered what I should say.

What did you say to the supposed love of your life?

Hey, how's it going? Long time since you ripped my heart out of my chest. But it's okay, I'm over it.

Sooner or later we had to meet again, but I had hoped I would have been better prepared. Especially because I wasn't over anything at all.

Seeing her face, knowing she didn't belong to me, sent a painful stab through my chest.

June and I looked into each other's eyes for a long time. Neither of us moved. The unmistakable tension between us crackled.

More and more emotions raged inside me.

Love. Hate. Anger. Sadness. Pain.

But there were also good memories. Our first dance. Our first kiss. Our first time having sex.

Finally, I was able to break free from the shock and entered the diner. At the same moment, June ran past me outside. I was enveloped by sweet lilac and quiet sobbing. Even after she had long since driven away in her light green city car, without saying a word.

Confused, I looked at Sue, who was looking at me knowingly.

"That was June Farley, wasn't it?" I asked.

"We both know that was June," Sue replied. She looked at me as if I were a little boy she had caught stealing.

She broke my heart, damn it!

"Did she say anything?" I asked further.

"Some things."

"Like what?" I could see how much Sue was enjoying keeping me in suspense.

"Oh, for example, about how much she likes New York."

"And how much does she like New York?"

Sue smiled at me lovingly, the way only my grandma could otherwise. "Why don't you finally ask me what you really want to know?"

I growled. "Did she say anything about me?"

"No."

I raised an eyebrow.

On one hand: Nice that June didn't have any bad words for me.

On the other hand: Ouch, that she had no words for me at all.

"Then why did you want me to ask about it?"

"Because otherwise the question would have hung in the air forever, and that ruins the appetite. So, what can I get you?"

I placed my order, sat down at an empty table, and waited patiently for my food while pondering why June still had so much power over me after all these years.

Because she still owns my damn heart. Even now.

"Here you go," Sue said, placing a large paper bag in front of me.

"Thanks."

But instead of leaving, Sue remained standing right in front of me.

"June will only be here for a short while. If you want to talk to her about anything, you'd better do it now."

"June just took off to New York. If she'd wanted to get in touch, she could have," I growled angrily.

Sue looked at me with the same expression as before. "She went to New York because of you, you idiot."

Damn small town. Even after years, my failed relationship with June was still a topic of conversation.

"Then I guess I'm an idiot," I grumbled. After that, I stood up and left the diner.

"She's staying at the main house on the Farley Ranch. Just in case you're not the big idiot we both think you are," Sue called after me.

I got into my car and drove angrily to Red Rivers.

Why couldn't the past just stay in the past and make room for the future? Because the past is the foundation of the future.

And I knew I'd royally screwed up laying that foundation. Maybe the reason I couldn't talk to June was because I'd have to face my own mistakes?

She had ripped my heart out of my chest and flung it all the way to New York, yes. But only because I was responsible for her heart shattering into a thousand pieces.

I wished things had gone differently.

Was there a cure for ripped out and broken hearts? And if so, what was the price?

"Heavens, John, there you are at last!" Elli gasped, before I even got out of the car. "I'm starving!"

Sophia was standing next to her. When the two stood side by side, they could be mistaken for twins. Elli was the spitting image of her older sister.

I got out of the car and distributed the food.

"What terrible conditions must prevail at Red Rivers for you to be almost starving?" I asked jokingly, and Elli giggled. But Sophia just sighed.

"If this drought continues, we'll really have a problem. Last year's crisis summer cost us a lot."

We leaned against the wooden fence that stood right next to the large horse stable and was used as a paddock, and unpacked our wrapped fast food.

"We'll find a solution," I said.

"Hopefully," Sophia replied and bit into her burger with extra bacon.

"Since when are you so pessimistic?" I asked thoughtfully.

Normally, Sophia was the sunshine of the family. She always had a smile on her lips and found a solution for everything. But most importantly: She never lost hope.

"Since we started operating in the red," she said quietly. Sophia had always had an organizational talent and had been taking care of Red Rivers' finances since she was fourteen. She didn't shy away from physical work either. She helped out wherever she was needed.

"I could maybe squeeze a few more horses into my schedule," Elli replied. She not only trained our own horses but also worked with horses from the surrounding area.

"You'd certainly have enough feed now," I said, nodding towards the truck.

"That would be a start. But I don't know if it's enough."

"What if I participate in a few competitions at the summer festival?"

Sophia and Elli looked at me equally astonished.

"Forget it, brother dear," Elli said, shaking her head.

Sophia nodded as well. "Riding a bronc is more for the younger guys. Better not, or you might break something."

I looked at Sophia threateningly. "I could show those young guys what a pro can do. Hasn't anyone told you that twenty-seven is the perfect age for rodeos?"

Years ago, I had won almost every rodeo ride and pocketed one prize money after another. Even if I didn't want to admit it, my sisters were right. I was too old. The last fall from a bronc had put me out of action for almost three months because I had broken my shoulder.

My grandma appeared from behind, carrying a large basket of red apples.

"You and your greasy fast food. Eat something healthy instead," she said reproachfully and threw me an apple, which I caught with my free hand.

"I'd rather wait until you make an apple pie out of it," I replied grinning and threw the apple back. Grandma sighed loudly, but she couldn't hide her grin from us.

Elli and Sophia giggled and each took an apple from the basket.

Of course they did. My two sisters had the long-blonde-curls bonus, being the only two girls, besides Mom and Grandma, on the farm. Otherwise, there was only me, my four brothers, three cousins, Dad, Grandpa, and Uncle Tim.

"Oh, have you heard?" Grandma asked, putting on her sensational reporter face.

"Heard what?" Sophia asked curiously, while Elli nodded.

I had the uneasy feeling that I already knew what the news was.

"Katy and Henry's granddaughter, June Farley, is back in town!"

"Oh, wow." Sophia looked at me, then Elli, then back at me. "Did you hear that, John?"

"I'm not deaf," I growled.

"What's she doing here? I thought she was super successful in New York?"

Grandma shrugged. "I don't know exactly. But Rosie saw her at the diner earlier."

"At the diner? When exactly earlier?" Sophia asked.

She shrugged again. "Sometime this afternoon."

"I see. This afternoon. John, you didn't happen to see June, did you?" Sophia looked at me reproachfully.

Great. Now my ancient love life was being rehashed by my family too.

"Maybe we crossed paths briefly."

"And what did she say?" Grandma, Elli, and Sophia asked simultaneously. I looked around, searching for male backup. But no one was in sight. Damn, usually at least three people would cross my path wanting something from me.

"Nothing. We didn't talk."

"Because you messed it up," Elli said, poking me in the chest with her index finger.

"Where is June staying, anyway?"

"In the main house of the Farley Ranch," I said absent-mindedly and immediately regretted it.

"I thought the Farleys sold their ranch long ago?" Grandma asked.

"Not entirely," I corrected. After June's grandparents died, her parents had sold almost all of the property to our neighbors. Just not the main house and the paddocks around it.

"We should invite June for dinner. She must be very lonely. And who knows if the Farley Ranch even has electricity right now. It's been uninhabited for months," Grandma mumbled to herself.

"What a great idea," Sophia cheered.

"If that's the case, I'll help you cook, Grandma," Elli offered.

I was outvoted. Great.

"You should invite June," Sophia encouraged me.

"I still have a lot to do. The fences on the east pasture need to be checked," I said.

"I can take care of that, no problem," Sophia replied sweetly. Unfortunately, it really wasn't a problem for Sophia. She could do a bit of everything, and when she wasn't handling finances or bureaucratic stuff, she helped out wherever she was needed.

"And the water troughs..." I continued searching for excuses.

"I'll clean them."

"And what if the road to the Farley Ranch isn't clear?"

Elli snapped her fingers excitedly and raised her hand like a schoolchild eager to solve a problem. "You could take the horses. The Farley Ranch is just a gallop away if you ride across the south pasture. And June would surely be happy to sit in a western saddle again. I don't think they have those on the East Coast."

"That sounds great."

"You can take Penny for that if you want. She's perfect for it," Sophia gushed about her horse. I hesitated briefly because although Penny was a good horse, she wouldn't have been my first choice.

"Penny? What about Champ?" I asked.

Sophia and Elli looked at each other, then pierced me with pitying glances.

"You shouldn't reopen old wounds," Sophia said gently.

I shouldn't reopen old wounds? June had already done that by disappearing - just like back then - without looking me in the eye.

"Whatever. If you want to see her for dinner, then invite her yourselves," I growled.

I really wasn't ready for another encounter with June. No idea if I'd ever be ready.

"John Theodore Joseph Key!" Grandma threatened with a raised finger. She had used my full name. That was never a good sign. "You will invite June to dinner and you will not come back without her, is that clear?"

"Yes, ma'am," I replied unhappily. When my grandma was in the mood for discussion - and she was when she called someone by their full name - it was better not to contradict her.

Chapter 3 – June

With an uneasy feeling, I drove down the road to my old home.

I had spent the first twenty years of my life here. Beautiful years that I missed. But I didn't miss how those years had ended.

It seemed almost like a cruel joke from the universe that Rachel and John were the first people I saw again in Merryville.

I had just managed to deal with Rachel, but when I saw John, tears welled up in my eyes faster than I would have liked, and I had to disappear. I had no other choice. I didn't want John to see that after all these years, I still had feelings for him. John had broken my heart, and he was the only one who could piece it back together. But there was no guarantee that he wouldn't destroy it again. I wouldn't survive this drama a second time.

The main house of the Farley Ranch appeared on the horizon and grew larger.

I parked the car and walked the rest of the way on foot to enjoy nature and the fresh air in the twilight. Nowhere in New York was the air as clean as it was here. Nowhere in New York did it smell so good of grass and home.

I loved the house my grandparents had left me. But the closer I got, the clearer it became that I could never sell the house in this condition. The windows were boarded up, the wooden facade was cracked and brittle, the dark brown paint had peeled off, and one could only imagine how beautiful the house had once been.

I unlocked the door and collapsed onto the dusty sofa in the living room. Fortunately, all the furniture, which now had a vintage charm, was intact and unharmed, just a bit dusty.

There was no electricity, nor water. Both had been shut off months ago because there had been a burst water pipe, the consequences of which had yet to be determined.

And yet I was happy to be here. I could have taken care of everything from afar, but I owed it to my grandparents to find a good owner for their land.

After resting for a moment, I took a walk through the farmhouse where I had grown up. Seeing it in this condition hurt.

Every step I took up the stairs creaked frighteningly, like in a horror movie.

Although I wasn't an architect, I knew that the damage from the burst pipe and the vacancy was extensive. Perhaps too extensive for a house in which four generations had grown up.

Lost in thought, I flipped through an old photo album I found in my grandparents' bedroom, then I heard a loud clattering from the kitchen and jumped.

"Hello?" I called downstairs.

Silence.

"Hello! Is anyone there?"

Silence again.

Of course! A burglar or horror movie villain wouldn't answer.

I summoned all my courage and slowly descended the stairs. The more I tried to be quiet, the louder the steps creaked.

One horror movie cliché chased the next and I was really getting worried.

There was another clatter, louder this time. Metal was being struck against metal.

"Hello?" I asked for the third time. A horror movie axe murderer wouldn't make such a racket. Slowly but surely, I approached the kitchen, searching for a usable weapon along the way. I found one in the form of an umbrella. Not ideal, but better than nothing.

"I'm armed," I called into the kitchen, as convincingly as I could. The unknown intruder continued clattering, unimpressed.

I took two deep breaths, then stormed into the kitchen, holding the umbrella like a spear. Except for an open cabinet from which the clattering was coming, I saw nothing.

Relieved, I lowered the umbrella, when suddenly a huge raccoon jumped out of the cabinet, and I screamed in fright. The raccoon ran into the laundry room, followed by its medium-sized raccoon family.

I watched the cute little animals that had given me the fright of my life and had to laugh at the unsuccessful theft attempt of the little ones.

That is, until I felt a hand on my shoulder and screamed again.

"Everything okay?"

I swung my umbrella to the side and caught John, who was standing behind me, on the upper arm. Although I had hit with full force, he only raised an eyebrow questioningly.

"Is it supposed to rain?" he asked amused, and I snorted loudly but said nothing. I wasn't in the mood for jokes when I looked into those hazel-brown, beautiful heartbreaker eyes.

John cleared his throat loudly. "Is everything okay?"

"Yes. Everything's great," I answered. "You just scared me to death. What are you doing here anyway?"

"I heard you scream and got worried."

I saw genuine concern on his face. As if John would sincerely worry about me. If he really cared about me, I would never have left Merryville.

"No, I mean, what are you doing on the Farley Ranch?" I asked further.

"Grandma invited you to dinner at Red Rivers."

I remembered Mary Key well, she had always been a role model for me, always so strong and confident.

"That's very kind of you, but I'm too busy," I politely declined. A dinner with John Key and his family was a true worst-case scenario for my feelings.

"Too busy with..." John asked and waited for an answer.

"With the house," I answered quickly.

"Hm." John looked around and grumbled once more. "Well, you won't be finished with it by this evening. Do you even have electricity? Or are you planning to roast marshmallows with your little guests over the fireplace later?"

I hated that John was making fun of me.

And I hated myself because I actually had to giggle.

"Well, the house has seen better days," I replied with a sigh. I definitely needed to hire an expert to take a look at the farmhouse.

"Damn right." John didn't even bother to sugarcoat the state of the house.

"Come on, nobody can say no to Grandma's meatloaf. And you definitely shouldn't sleep in a dilapidated house full of wild animals."

"I have a car," I defended myself.

"And Red Rivers has five houses full of guest rooms."

No way.

"Okay, I'll accept your dinner invitation. But nothing more."

"Fine, I can live with that."

And how can you live with having broken my heart?

I followed John outside and had expected a pickup truck or a motorcycle, but not two horses peacefully grazing in front of my front door.

When he saw my questioning face, he answered, "Riding across the south fields is faster than driving."

"Okay," I said meekly. It had been ages since I'd last sat on a horse.

John pulled a pair of western boots from the saddlebag of his black gelding and set them down in front of me.

"Be careful, they belong to Sophia. She loves these things. All four hundred pairs she owns."

As much as I wanted to hate John, he still made me laugh, and it felt like he was slowly but surely picking up the pieces of my heart.

After I had swapped my ballerina flats for Sophia's boots, John handed me the reins of the second horse.

"This is Penny, Sophia's horse."

"Wow, what a beauty. Hello Penny," I greeted the white and brown pinto horse. I took the reins from John and stroked Penny's neck.

"She sure is."

Thoughtfully, I bit my lip while continuing to stroke the soft coat.

"What is it?" John asked.

"It's been forever since I last sat on a horse."

"Aren't there horses in New York?"

"There are. But that kind of society is more Rachel's thing," I answered contemptuously. There, neither fun nor character mattered, only pedigrees and blue ribbons.

Not to mention, I was far from over Champion. Back then, we had won almost every ribbon, medal, and trophy there was to win in the region. I missed Champ.

"Oh, my condolences. But with Penny, you don't need to worry, she's a calm horse. Perfect for beginners."

"Okay, now I feel insulted. I'm not a beginner," I snorted.

"Then you're just avoiding the saddle for fun?"

I snorted loudly, then placed my foot in the wide stirrup and swung myself up. John, standing behind me, held my hips for safety, and for a moment, time stood still. His hands on my body triggered feelings I had long kept locked away. It felt good, but it had felt good back then too, before...

"See, not a beginner." I took up the reins and enjoyed the world from a rider's perspective. This was by far what I had missed the most. Leisurely rides and cattle driving. I would have even given up my cutting career to escape the cruel reality.

"I'll believe that when you stay in the saddle all the way to Red Rivers," John said laughing and mounted his gelding, which he introduced to me as Copper.

"If anyone falls off their horse - or their high horse - it'll be you," I said, as dryly as I could.

"Damn it, stop holding that against me," John growled. "That was a lifetime ago."

John was right, it was a lifetime ago.

"What do you mean?" I asked, giggling innocently.

"You know exactly what I mean!"

I burst out laughing. "Yes, that's right. I remember your two-second ride well. But I remember even better that I won."

When I thought about my youth, this was the number two experience that came to mind. When I had bet John that I could stay on the wild black rodeo horse longer than he could. I was the only girl and, to everyone's surprise, I had masterfully survived the eight-second ride and won. It was the first and only time I had participated in a rodeo.

John gritted his teeth and his jaw muscles tensed as he eyed me seriously. He had never given me such a look before. So full of anger and passion and something I couldn't quite define. All I knew was that I had to protect myself from these looks because they attracted me.

"Yeah, yeah, Miss Pride-Comes-Before-a-Fall, shall we ride now?" John asked and urged Copper on.

"Alright, Mr. I'm-a-Sore-Loser," I replied and clicked my tongue. At the same time, I hoped he wouldn't make any more jokes or give me another one of those exciting looks, because otherwise I might forget that I actually hated John.

Chapter 4 – John

As I helped June into the saddle, our eyes met and something flashed in her emerald green eyes. Something she wanted to hide, but couldn't. It lasted less than a second, but it was enough to know that June still loved me. Just as I still loved her. But we were both too stubborn, too proud, and too hurt to admit it.

We continued to stare at each other, neither of us daring to say anything.

Clearing my throat, I removed my hand, which was still on her perfect waist, and then I did the dumbest thing I could have done. I patted her bare calf as if she were a buddy and silently walked over to Copper, who was nibbling on some withered blades of grass.

"Ready?" I asked, adjusting my cowboy hat.

"Ready," June answered quietly and followed me.

"What are you planning to do with the Farley Ranch?" I asked to break the silence between us.

"Sell it, I guess," June replied with a shrug. I let my gaze sweep over the dilapidated house, the rickety barn, the rusty tractor, the weeds everywhere.

"Then you'll have a lot to do before anyone buys it from you," I said thoughtfully.

"I know," June sighed.

"It's a shame everything's fallen into such disrepair."

"I should have come earlier, then maybe I could have saved something," June said bitterly.

I cleared my throat. "Sorry, that wasn't meant as a reproach."

"No, it's okay. You're right. My grandparents would be tearing their hair out if they knew what happened to the Farley Ranch."

It broke my heart to see June like this. Doubt and self-reproach were eating her up from the inside.

"I'm sure they understand... everything."

June smiled at me painfully. "Certainly."

"You could also live here again yourself," I suggested. "Henry and Katy would surely like that."

A part of me would too.

"No way," June answered a bit too quickly. "I mean, I live in New York now. And how am I supposed to make money with a farm without farmland? My parents sold almost everything."

"Buy it back," I said with a shrug. That's when my grandma's naive pragmatism, which she had passed down to almost every Key, came through in me.

"A nice thought. But I can't." June sighed heavily, and I wondered why she couldn't. Or if she just didn't want to come.

As oppressive silence threatened to develop between us again, June's stomach growled so loudly that even our horses pricked up their ears.

June's cheeks colored with embarrassment, and she looked at me apologetically.

"Apart from Sue's apple crumble pie, I haven't had a proper meal today."

"Then we should ride a little faster. Don't want you taking a bite out of Penny, you've been looking at her funny this whole time," I joked, and June laughed.

"Thanks, I'll pass and wait for your grandma's meatloaf. If it's even half as good as I remember, it'll be the best roast in years."

"Trust me, it's gotten even better."

"What are we waiting for then?" June asked, then galloped ahead with Penny. Her black dress fluttered in the wind, revealing tantalizing areas that made me think thoughts I could feel not only in my head.

I wanted to enjoy the sight for a while longer, but unfortunately, my horse hated losing just as much as I did. So a race broke out between June and me that wasn't decided until the end of Red River's south pasture.

"So, which one of us is the beginner now?" June asked laughing.

"Still you. Copper and I let you win."

"You're still just as bad a loser as you were back then," June giggled.

She was right. I was a damn bad loser. And it had driven me half crazy to lose June, because she was the only woman I ever really wanted. And even now, after she had shredded my heart, I still wanted her.

I studied her face, which had become even more beautiful in the meantime, and her long brown hair that reached down to her breasts.

"Is something wrong?" June asked thoughtfully after I had stared at her for too long. Her eyes widened. "Is there a spider on me somewhere?"

Immediately she dropped the reins and patted her body for potential crawling critters before I could reassure her.

"No, there's no spider."

"A horsefly?"

I shook my head. "No."

"Then why were you staring at me?" June asked, furrowing her brow.

Because you're so beautiful that I can't stop admiring you.

"I was lost in thought, nothing more," I lied. "We're almost there." I pointed to our main house and the barns, which we could see clearly from the south pasture, then we rode on.

Just before the yard, June stopped and sighed loudly.

"What's wrong?" I asked.

"I'm looking forward to seeing your family, really."

"But?"

"But I don't want you to tell them about the poor condition of the Farley Ranch. Your grandma would immediately try to find a place for me to stay."

"Not just my grandma," I said. There was no way I would let June stay overnight in that house. The water damage could have affected the structural integrity, not to mention the raccoon gang. If they could get into the house unnoticed, so could rattlesnakes or bears. No. I wouldn't allow June to stay in that house under any circumstances.

"Please. I don't want to cause any trouble."

June, you've already managed that...

"Don't worry about it and just enjoy dinner, okay?" I winked at her.

"Okay."

In the yard, Elli came to meet us, offering to help with the horses, selfless as she was. Not. I knew exactly that she and Sophia were just itching to analyze every little detail between June and me. The two of them lived in a fantasy world with utopian ideas about true first love and second chances. As if Sophia would simply stumble into her Mr.

Right, or Elli would meet the love of her life through her love of horses. No, life doesn't work that way.

"So, how was the ride?" Elli asked.

"Great," June replied, beaming from ear to ear. Then she leaned forward and whispered in a half-loud voice: "I beat John in a race, but don't rub it in his face, okay?" Both of them giggled.

"No, I would never rub it in John's face when he loses at something. These things happen. To some less often and to others - like John - more often." Elli's giggle turned into loud laughter.

"I can see you're fine on your own," I growled, then followed the smell of roast and vegetables into the main house.

June ran after me and looked at me apologetically.

"I'm sorry. They were just a few jokes."

"It's fine. Everyone loves jokes at their expense."

June looked at me. "How can I make it up to you?"

Promise me you'll stay here, marry me, and raise five beautiful children with me.

Damn, just for having that thought I longed for an ice-cold shower. The heat, which still made the horizon shimmer even in the evening, must have gone to my head.

"Next time, remind me not to let you win," I answered with a wink. Then we strolled leisurely into the kitchen of the main house, where my grandma was just taking the meatloaf out of the oven and hugged June exuberantly when she saw us.

"Welcome, dear. Make yourself at home."

"Thank you so much for the invitation."

Grandma took a step back and looked June up and down, who nervously smoothed her black dress.

"You look great. Like a real city woman."

"With awesome shoes," Sophia called out as she was setting the table.

I only needed half a glance at the good china, which was usually only brought out at Christmas, to know what was going on.

"Pretty small gathering. Where is everyone?"

"Hm?" Sophia asked, tilting her head as she always did when she wanted to appear innocent. "What do you mean, brother dear?"

"Where are the other two-thirds of our family eating?" I asked more clearly this time.

"At Sue's. Grandpa invited everyone."

"Did he?" I raised an eyebrow and looked at Grandma, who was placing the meatloaf on a serving platter.

June became embarrassed again. "I didn't want to cause any trouble."

"No, you're not! It's wonderful to have you here, June."

"Thank you, I'm glad to be back here too. What's new?"

Sophia waved it off. "Believe me, even if you haven't been here for years, you're still up to date. Absolutely nothing has happened. But I'm sure a lot has happened in New York, right? You have to tell me everything about New York."

Sophia's eyes lit up when she mentioned New York. Ever since she had seen her first movie set in the Big Apple as a child, she had been fascinated by the city.

I put Grandma's legendary meatloaf on the table and Sophia brought grilled vegetables and salad.

We ate while June was grilled alternately by Sophia and Elli about life in the big city. June smiled the whole time as she talked about her life in the metropolis, but I could see that this smile wasn't genuine. Whatever she had experienced on the East Coast, she didn't want to drag it back to Merryville.

I pondered for so long about whether June was running from something, and why she felt safe from it here of all places, until Elli snapped me out of my thoughts with a question.

"It's so late, do you want to sleep here tonight?"

Chapter 5 – June

Dinner at the Keys' was great, even though I had to do a song and dance about my failed career. I didn't want anyone to worry. I didn't want pity. And above all, I didn't want mockery. A failed cowgirl in the big city was just too cliché.

John watched me the whole time and caught me looking at him repeatedly. Something had happened between us that I couldn't quite describe. The spark between us had never gone out, even after years apart.

But he had broken my heart. And I had simply run away. A series of mistakes and misunderstandings that couldn't be undone.

I was just telling them about the ice-cold winters when Elli asked:

"It's so late, do you want to sleep here tonight?"

I looked reproachfully at John. He raised his hands in a placating gesture, silently telling me that he hadn't said anything about the condition of the Farley Ranch.

"That's really very kind..." I began, then Mrs. Key interrupted me.

"It is. So kind that you can't refuse. The guest bed is already made up, and John can drive you back to the Farley Ranch tomorrow."

John's grandma had always had the gift of making things palatable that you hated.

"Okay," I sighed. "But at least let me help you with your work. I haven't been in a stable for years."

"You can help me feed the horses," Elli offered, and I nodded. "Gladly."

Sophia cleared her throat. "Let John do that. Or have you forgotten... that thing?"

"What thing?" Elli asked.

"You know, that super important thing I need your help with. Now."

"Oh, that thing! Of course. John?"

John growled softly, and I tried to smile away the sisters' less-than-subtle action.

After dinner, we all took care of the dishes together, and I chatted with John's grandma about old times.

The longer I stayed at Red Rivers, the bigger the question became of why I had left in the first place. I loved the land, the people, the ranch work, I loved every single day I had spent in Merryville.

"Thank you, dear. But the horses are getting hungry," Mrs. Key said with a wink and took the plate I was drying from me. Admittedly, I hadn't exactly hurried with the dishes to stall for time.

John and me, alone in the stable? That could only go wrong. Either because I couldn't control my old feelings and we'd argue, or because I couldn't control my old feelings and we'd suddenly find ourselves naked in the hay. Neither was an option. My heart had been through enough, and I still needed it in New York... for whatever reason.

The land I loved was here.

The life I loved could only be lived here.

The love of my life was here.

"Thanks, I'll go then," I said with a smile.

John was leaning casually against the big barn door, waiting for me. He was still as attractive as ever. Even more so. His broad shoulders seemed even broader, and the stubble that covered his chiseled cheeks made him look even more masculine. Then I remembered the glint in his eyes that I had never seen before and couldn't get out of my head.

My core, which had never betrayed me before, tingled and pulsed when I thought of that look.

"Ready?" John asked with a meaningful glance that made it clear he didn't mean the feeding. He was asking if I was ready to venture into the lion's den.

"Yes," I answered with a smile, trying to hide my fear. He handed me several buckets that smelled of cornflakes, herbs, and fresh carrots. I placed them in a row in the front stalls. Immediately, chewing sounds joined the snorting and hoof-pawing.

"Done," I said contentedly and clapped my dusty hands.

Then I went to the stall where John was hanging up a full hay net. I immediately recognized the horse that was contentedly nibbling on some loose hay ends.

Champion of Tournament. My Champ.

John looked at me seriously over the stall door.

"I'm sorry, I didn't know how to tell you."

Tears welled up in my eyes. Leaving Champ behind had been just as hard as leaving John.

"You bought Champ?"

John nodded.

"Why?" I asked softly.

"Because I thought you'd come back for him." He stroked Champ's caramel-colored coat. "We both hoped you'd come back. Every single day."

That was the most honest thing John had said since my arrival. No stupid jokes. No silence. Just real feelings.

"Here I am," I whispered.

"And how long will you stay?" John asked.

"As long as I can," I answered.

I opened the stall door, stepped in, and stroked Champ's soft nostrils. He looked great. His caramel-colored coat was shiny, and his blonde mane shimmered like silk.

"Hey Champ," I said softly, and he nibbled on my fingertips. "John? Why didn't you tell me earlier that you bought Champ?"

"I didn't know if I'd be reopening old wounds."

You already have... even without Champ.

"Thank you for giving him a good home. Does Elli take him to competitions?"

Champ was the best cutting horse in all of Texas, he loved his job, and I loved him.

"At first, yes. But he hasn't been the same since you left."

"Nobody's been the same since I left," I replied thoughtfully.

"True." John's voice was rough, raspy, and irresistible. The longer I stood so close to him, the less I could resist him. Especially now, with my heart unprotected and open, and his hazel eyes promising comfort.

I meant something to John, otherwise he would never have kept Champ for so long. It was the most beautiful thing that could have happened to me. At the same time, it was also the worst, because it destroyed my illusion of the heartbreaking cowboy without feelings.

"I missed you," I whispered. Words my heart spoke before my head could stop them.

John looked at me intently, and the air between us began to crackle with tension.

"And I thought about you every single day," he replied honestly.

Why couldn't we have spoken so candidly years ago? Maybe everything would have turned out differently.

"Why did it all go so terribly wrong back then?" I asked, tears in my eyes.

"You were too scared, and I was too proud," John answered.

Then he grabbed me by the shoulders and pressed me against the wooden wall. He pushed his body against mine and I let out a soft moan.

"What are you doing?" I gasped as his lips touched my neck.

I wanted more of it.

I wanted him to stop.

I wanted him to continue.

I wanted everything.

"What I should have done years ago. Hold you tight."

Then our lips met and the electricity between us intensified massively. Sparks flew, I felt hot, and my whole body tingled. His hands gripped my shoulders with firm pressure. I could barely move, but I liked it. He held me so tightly that I felt secure, safe, protected.

"Damn, June. I missed you so much," John murmured. Then that something flickered in his eyes again, the same look that had made me pensive earlier. But this time it didn't fade. This time I understood what that look was saying.

You belong to me.

And then there was my heart, answering:

I want to belong to you.

Then I hesitated.

"What are we doing, John?" I asked again.

"The right thing. What we should have done long ago."

"No, we shouldn't be doing this," I sighed. I wanted to feel him. I wanted his kisses, his touches, his love. But I didn't want to risk my heart a second time, because I was still busy picking up the pieces that John had left behind.

I allowed one last, bittersweet kiss, then I pushed John away, whispered "I can't do this," and did what I did best. I ran.

Lost in thought, I sipped coffee on the veranda of the main house at Red Rivers. It was a beautiful morning, the sun rising with a rich red into the sky, and the horses and cows grazing peacefully in the pasture.

Nature was acting as if the worst-case scenario for my feelings hadn't occurred last night.

That was one of the reasons why I had waited in the guest room for John to leave with his brothers and Elli for the northern pasture to drive the cattle back to the nearer fields. What had happened between us last night couldn't happen again. No way! I had to protect my small, naive, completely shattered heart. I had to resist John! But that was hardly possible with John's glances, John's rough voice, his masculine scent and his broad shoulders. That's why I had chosen the coward's method, I was hiding.

"Good morning," said Sophia, beaming as brightly as the sun.

"Good morning," I replied.

"Sleep well?"

"Great," I lied. I hadn't slept a wink all night.

"Guess who's the second-worst liar in the whole world?" Sophia asked with a wink.

"Hmm. Good question," I said, pretending Sophia hadn't caught me lying.

"It must not be easy for you to be back here," Sophia said empathetically.

I shook my head. "No. It sounds absurd, but it feels easy. The only thing that feels hard is the fact that I wasn't here for so long."

"I understand exactly what you mean. I love Red Rivers more than anything too..." Sophia said, then paused.

"Sounds like there's a 'but' coming," I said.

"But," she began, grinning, "it feels like something's missing. I don't know exactly what. I just know that I'll know it when I find it. Does that make sense?"

I smiled at Sophia. "That makes absolute sense!"

"Maybe I'll find my happiness in New York? Who knows," Sophia mused. "But my happiness will probably have to wait a while for me."

"Why?" I asked.

"I can't leave Red Rivers alone. Not now."

"Are you having problems?"

Sophia nodded. "All of Merryville is having problems because of the drought. This is the second hottest summer in two decades. And we had the hottest summer last year. It will take years before all the fields can be cultivated again. And the water for our cattle is slowly running low, but we can't afford a water tank because we've been in the red for months."

"How terrible. If I can help you, let me know. I'll help where I can." I empathized with Sophia. No, I empathized with all of Merryville - my home.

"Thank you, but don't worry. We've overcome every crisis so far, this time won't be any different. Back to you, June. Did you find what you were looking for in New York?"

I shook my head. "No, unfortunately not."

"Really not?"

I pondered what to answer. Because before this conversation, I had never really been aware that I could never see my refuge as anything other than a refuge.

"I worked, worked, worked. So long until I was one of the most successful interior designers in all of New York."

"But that sounds great, doesn't it?" Sophia asked, confused.

"True, but I didn't want to decorate two-hundred-million-dollar villas with loveless, super-expensive stuff. I never wanted that."

"So what do you want?"

"To create a home. A place where you want to stay forever."

Over the years, I had furnished so many apartments in search of a home and never realized that I could only be at home at home.

As if struck by lightning, I jumped up. Thanks to Sophia, I had a brilliant idea that I had to pursue immediately.

"Could you please take me to the Farley Ranch? And we need a pen and paper. Lots of paper!"

"Is everything alright?" Sophia asked worriedly.

"Yes, everything's fine!"

Sophia got everything from the main house, though quite puzzled, and then we set off while I explained my plan to her.

Chapter 6 – John

Listlessly, I drove part of the cattle towards the farm. Elli was busy trying to calm her horse, which kept trying to break free. We had to lead the animals closer to our main house because all the water sources outside had dried up due to the heat. Red Rivers couldn't afford to lose its livestock under any circumstances. I had other things to do as well, but as it looked, we would be occupied with driving the herd for quite a while. More accurately, I was busy driving the cattle back, while Elli had her hands full trying to keep Phoenix under control.

When Elli saw my annoyed look, she said with full conviction: "Trust me, Phoenix will become a great ranch horse."

"He's afraid of cows," I replied dryly.

My sister had been working with Phoenix for weeks. The white horse was beautiful, no question, but in my eyes, a hopeless case. She often worked with horses from the area, trained ranch horses, and turned problematic beasts into docile ponies, and she did it very well. But a ranch horse that was afraid of cattle was a pretty difficult case.

"He's not quite comfortable with them yet," Elli admitted through gritted teeth. "But it's getting better every day. And before you know it, Phoenix will be a first-class ranch horse."

"You should be careful not to trip over your boundless optimism," I growled.

"What happened between you and June?" Elli asked.

"Nothing. What could have happened between us?" I lied.

"Normally, you'd be cracking one joke after another - a ranch horse being herded by cows, or something like that - but you're grumbling in a bad mood, and your face looks like three days of rainy weather."

My sister was right, but I would never admit it. What happened last night was nobody's business.

Damn, I had waited for June all morning to talk to her about our kiss. But she had barricaded herself in her room until I had to go to work.

"Rain is what we need most urgently right now," I sighed and listened to the dry grass crackling under Copper's hooves.

"True. Red Rivers desperately needs rain. And you desperately need couples therapy."

I brought Copper to a halt. "What?"

"You and June. You still love each other, there's no doubt about that. You're both just too stubborn or too scared to talk about it."

"If you say so, Professor Doctor Key," I grumbled.

"Yes, I do say so."

Our conversation was interrupted by Phoenix shying away because a curious calf had come too close to him.

I kept thinking about the kiss I had let myself be carried away with. Never had a woman turned my head like June. She was everywhere. I could hear her voice in the gentle breeze as I breathed in the lilac-scented air.

"What are you going to do?" Elli asked when she had Phoenix under control again. My sister really had the patience of a saint with this hopeless case.

"Nothing."

"Nothing?"

"Nothing," I repeated, shrugging my shoulders.

"You're going to let her go to New York a second time?" Elli snorted loudly. "You idiot."

I paused because I hadn't even thought about that yet. June would leave Merryville again sooner or later. She would leave me again. And she would drag my damn heart across the states a second time.

If June did that, I would definitely be a broken man, no question.

"What do you think I should do?" I asked, without admitting that Elli was right.

"Spend time with her and remind her where her home is."

"Her home is in New York now. What does Merryville have to offer that New York doesn't?"

I shook my head as I realized I was trying to compete with a huge city.

"You," Elli answered seriously, and I laughed.

"Me? You remember that June went to New York in the first place because of me?"

"Yes. But the circumstances are different this time. Don't let her go a second time."

"Easier said than done."

"What happened between you two?" Elli asked a second time.

I raised an eyebrow and said, "That stays between us."

Elli raised her right hand and turned her palm towards me. "Indian's honor."

"I kissed her yesterday."

Now Elli's jaw dropped. "Really?"

"Yes. After I told her I missed her."

"Did she miss you too?"

"Damn right, she did. Otherwise, I wouldn't have kissed her in the first place."

Elli clapped her hands in excitement.

"That's great, John. Why are you in such a bad mood then?"

"Because she ran away afterward." Saying my rejection out loud scratched at my pride. I had always been a ladies' man, but my heart had always belonged only to June. She was the perfect woman - there was no topping that - and no one could hold a candle to her.

Elli seemed little surprised by my answer, which surprised me.

"You seem very astonished," I growled as Elli just looked at me with pity.

"What did you expect? Of course, her feelings are in turmoil. You broke her heart years ago, and now she's afraid it will happen again."

"She broke my heart just as much," I replied grumpily.

Snorting, Elli tilted her head back. "John, this isn't a competition. But you have to make a decision."

"Between what?" I asked.

"Between the past and the future. What happened then has happened and can't be undone. But you can decide now how your future will look. Do you want June back?"

"Absolutely."

"Then accept that her feelings are confused. Give her time and show her how you feel about her."

I nodded. Who would have thought I could still learn something from my little sister? I was grateful to Elli for listening to my problems, and her prognosis didn't look as gloomy as I had feared. On the other hand, she was giving this cow-phobic horse a chance. I gave Phoenix a serious look.

Either we were both hopeless cases that my sister was breaking her teeth on, or she believed in us because she saw something that was hidden from others.

There was still one question that had tormented me for years and had been driving me half crazy since our kiss.

"And what if she doesn't feel the same anymore?"

Elli giggled. Unbelievable. She giggled while we were having the most serious conversation ever.

"You would have noticed that right after the kiss if she had whacked you with a pitchfork. Joking aside. I've seen the looks you've been giving each other. There's absolutely no doubt that she still loves you."

"And do you think she can ever forgive me for my mistake?" I asked. Damn, I had destroyed my life in two seconds back then.

Instead of answering me, Elli asked me a counter-question.

"Can you forgive her for being away for so long?"

Without hesitation, I nodded, and Elli smiled at me.

"Then she can forgive you too."

Satisfied, we continued driving the cattle until we reached our destination and I spotted a dust cloud on the horizon moving in our direction. No one in our family would have pushed the pickup truck that hard. Red paint shimmered through the swirling dust.

"Are we expecting someone?" I asked thoughtfully.

"Not that I know of," Elli replied.

As the car slowed down when it was at eye level, we rode to the boundary fence to see what was going on.

"Oh, we're getting a high-profile visitor," Elli said disparagingly as Rachel Pearson got out of the car. She was the last person I needed right now. I hadn't forgotten that Rachel was actually to blame for all my problems.

Still, I had to rein in my sister.

"Don't say that too loud. The Pearsons will soon be the only ones with green grass left," I pressed through my clenched teeth.

"As if they'd let anything other than half-million-dollar nags on their luxury polo lawn," Elli replied half-seriously, and I gave her a warning look.

"Okay, okay. I'll be quiet."

Rachel walked around her red Ferrari, took off her oversized Prada sunglasses, and pushed them up onto her forehead.

"Hello!" she called out and leaned her upper body over the wooden fence. "What a coincidence, I was looking for you two specifically."

"And found us," Elli said, grinning broadly, before looking at me questioningly. I shrugged my shoulders because I had no idea what Rachel was doing here. She hadn't set foot on Red Rivers in years.

"Rachel." I tipped the brim of my cowboy hat and nodded to her.

"What's up?" Elli asked curiously.

"I have a problem with one of my horses. Could you take a look at it?"

"What?" Elli asked, surprised. "I thought you had your own trainers."

"I do. But they're all busy. And if Citizen Silver doesn't start winning ribbons again soon..." Rachel didn't finish her sentence because we all knew how the Pearsons dealt with horses that no longer made a profit.

"Sure, I can take a look at your horse, but I don't usually work with show jumpers. And I don't have much time at the moment."

Of course, we were always busy with something on Red Rivers, but I knew why Elli was really declining. She didn't want to cause any more problems with Rachel sneaking around the ranch. But how likely was it that she would set foot on our ranch? She hadn't been here in years. Still, I found the timing anything but good.

Rachel pulled out her checkbook, wrote down a number, tore out the page, and handed it to Elli, whose eyes grew quite large.

"I'll pay in advance, of course. When can I bring Citizen Silver over?" Rachel asked, ignoring Elli's refusal.

"Um," Elli began. Then I cleared my throat and took the check from her, which had a sum written on it that we couldn't possibly turn down. We needed this money to save Red Rivers. Our ranch was more important than my pride.

"I can take over some of your tasks," I offered Elli, signaling that she had to accept the damn check.

Elli sighed softly, and her gaze shifted back and forth between the check and me.

"Alright. But I can't promise I can help. As I said, I rarely work with show jumpers," Elli emphasized once again.

"If you're even half as good as your reputation, you'll manage it easily," Rachel said sweetly. "So, when should I bring Citizen Silver over? This afternoon?"

"Sounds good," Elli replied.

"Great. Then we'll see you later." Rachel put her black sunglasses back on, which covered half her face, and was already on her way back when I asked:

"Haven't you forgotten something?"

"What?" Rachel asked, irritated.

"You tell me. You said earlier you wanted to see Elli and me."

"Oh!" Rachel put on a fake, broad smile. "I just wanted to say hello to you because we haven't seen each other in so long."

And there was a damn good reason for that.

I wasn't just ignoring her because I knew women like Rachel couldn't handle being ignored and would become twice as annoying.

"Ah," I replied. "Hello."

"Hiii," Rachel said, drawing it out so long that she sounded like a little cowgirl meeting Bonnie Buckley, the greatest country star who ever lived.

Elli said nothing, but I knew my sister well enough to know that all her alarm bells were ringing in bright red.

"We still have a lot to do and need to get going now. So, see you this afternoon," Elli saved us all from the awkward situation.

"See you then!" Rachel said goodbye, got into her car, and rushed off just as quickly as she had arrived.

"What the hell was that?" Elli asked.

"I have no idea," I answered honestly. Even though I didn't want to admit that the check had just saved our asses...

"The check just saved our asses."

"Let's hope Citizen Silver cooperates, or that check will bounce faster than you can say rodeo," Elli replied with a sigh.

On the way back to the ranch, I noticed a shaggy, brown spot.

"We forgot a calf," I grumbled, knowing full well that I'd have to drive it back to the herd. Elli scanned the pasture and shook her head.

"I don't think it's a calf."

"What else could it be?" I asked.

"Let's take a look."

Fearlessly, Elli drove the white scaredy-horse towards the unknown animal, and I followed her. The closer we got, the clearer the animal's horns became, and the characteristic bleating of a goat.

"Where did you come from?" Elli asked, but she got no answer.

"Is there even a farm with goats in Merryville?" I asked. I didn't know of anyone within thirty miles who kept goats. The little beasts could devour more hay than a starving herd of cows and not infrequently ate the hair right off their owners' heads. Most farmers around here specialized in cattle, sheep, or pigs.

"No idea. Let's take her back to the farm for now, then we'll see. Maybe our little runaway is sorely missed somewhere."

Since Phoenix showed no signs of fear, Elli swung her lasso and easily caught the goat.

We rode together, with the goat in tow, back to the ranch. I hoped to see June somewhere. Elli was right, we needed to talk about the past, put it behind us so we could start anew. Damn it, this time I wouldn't just let June go. Even if I had to catch her with a lasso!

Just before the main house, we saw Sophia, who was riding towards the south pasture. When she noticed us, she turned around and galloped straight towards us. There was a crazy gleam in her eyes that scared me. That's exactly how crazy cat ladies looked at every cat that crossed their path.

"Hey," Sophia began excitedly. "I think I've found a way to turn our red numbers black again!"

"You too?" Elli asked, confused.

"What do you mean, me too?" Sophia replied, puzzled. "What do you want with the goat anyway?"

She pointed at our tagalong.

"We caught her in the pasture," I answered.

"Oh, how cute," Sophia squealed and petted the friendly goat. "I think she needs a name."

Elli nodded. "Definitely! Anyone have any ideas?"

"Goat," I said dryly.

"How about Nougat?" Sophia suggested.

"Because of her nougat-colored fur?"

"And because you can eat nougat too?" I teased them. Of course, I knew the goat wouldn't end up in any of our stews.

"John!" Elli looked at me reproachfully. Then she beamed again. "Nougat sounds great. Welcome to Red Rivers, Nougat!"

I sighed quietly.

Sophia, who couldn't get enough of the little goat, looked at me.

"You have news. Tell me about it so I can finally tell you my news, I'm about to burst with excitement!"

"Rachel Pearson wrote Elli a check to work with one of her horses," I explained to Sophia.

"Rachel Pearson?" Sophia asked.

"Yep. We had the same look on our faces," Elli said. "And what's your plan?"

Immediately, Sophia got that cat-lady gleam again that scared me.

"My plan, well, actually June's plan, is brilliant. And it would solve all our problems."

Sophia's stories sounded too good to be true.

"Did you discover an oil deposit we didn't know about? Or a gold vein?" I asked.

"Better!"

I got an uneasy feeling. Sophia was always in a good mood, but now she was downright manic, in a creepy way.

"Better?" Elli and I asked in unison.

"Much better! There's just one problem."

My uneasy feeling grew stronger.

"And that would be?"

"We need to convince June to stay longer. Without her, we can't pull it off."

Elli and Sophia looked at me equally threateningly, telepathically screaming something like: "Don't screw this up!" or "Get it together!"

June, the cause of all my problems, was supposed to be the salvation for Red Rivers?

Chapter 7 – June

I CRITICALLY EXAMINED MY grandparents' house where I had grown up. Sophia and I had hatched a grand plan that we wanted to implement as soon as possible.

I firmly believed in our project, even though it was associated with a lot of heartache for two reasons.

First, because the structural engineer who had just been here declared the ranch house in danger of collapse. The water damage had affected the foundation so much that we couldn't save it.

And second, the plan wouldn't work without John's help.

I glanced at John, who was casually leaning against his truck and talking on the phone. Unfortunately, the plan required me to spend a lot of time with John. More than I liked and more than was good for both of us.

John ended his call and came towards me.

"Sophia was able to find someone who can take another look at the house tomorrow."

"Wow," I replied, full of admiration. Sophia had promised to find a second expert as quickly as possible to take another look at my grandparents' house. Not that I didn't believe the first structural engineer... but I hoped he was wrong.

I had grown up in this small, dark brown wooden house. The mere thought of having to tear it down was very painful. Nowhere else did I have anything that came as close to home as here.

It became quiet between John and me again.

Since the kiss last night, there had been an unmistakable tension between us, which I tried to avoid. At the same time, his hazel magnetic eyes kept drawing me in. The silence made me uncomfortable and I fiddled with the hem of my yellow polka dot summer dress that reached just above my knees. I was still wearing Sophia's western boots.

I cleared my throat to distract myself from my thoughts. "What do you actually think about our idea?"

Although John had agreed to help us, he hadn't said anything else about it.

"Hm." He put his hands in his pockets and kicked a few pebbles. "It could be good."

"Could be? Do you have so little faith in your sister? It's going to be great."

John looked at me meaningfully, and I knew it wasn't about a lack of trust in his sister.

"Do you even have enough time for the project? You have a job with obligations and a life in New York."

I tried not to show the pain that John's doubts had caused.

"Don't worry, I'll stay until everything is up and running."

"I hope you mean it," John said dryly.

"I mean it very seriously," I answered with conviction.

I really did mean it. Even though I was a world champion at running away from problems, I would never turn my back on this project because I loved this land. It was my home. And I wanted to share this home with others. That's why I had proposed a deal to Sophia that she could never refuse.

I would provide my land and my savings, while they would take care of the construction and maintenance. Together we would create the most beautiful vacation ranch in the world from scratch. We would create a home away from home, and it felt right. For the first time in years, I felt good. The decision I had made was right, I knew that for sure.

"It feels right. That's why it will work," I said dreamily. I smiled confidently at John and forgot for a second that we still hadn't talked about the kiss. On one hand, I wanted more kisses, more touches, more John. On the other hand, I wanted to finally close the chapter on my past and years of heartache.

The looks between us sparked again, and I felt betrayed by my body, which longed for John's closeness. To avoid falling for him a second time, I pulled a few long plastic posts from the bed of the truck to mark off a few spots in the grass next to the ranch.

"A vacation house should stand here," I said and marked out a rectangle.

John followed suit and got more posts. "And here?"

He seemed less confident than I was, but I smiled contentedly.

"Perfect," I said.

"Perfect?" John repeated. "A little crooked, I'd say."

I shrugged. "Doesn't matter. We only need perfection and a measuring stick when we know exactly where the vacation houses should be built."

"Still crooked," John teased with a grin, which elicited a loud snort from me. I stood between two posts. "Here's the entrance." Then I entered the house. "And this will be the open bedroom, where the first rays of the sun will shine directly through the window. And at the fireplace that will be here, you can roast marshmallows and drink hot chocolate in the evening. And over here is the bathroom, with a large, freestanding bathtub from which you can see the horses grazing on the south paddock."

The more I explained, the more real my vision felt. Yes, I even had the feeling of standing in the finished apartment.

John watched me with every step. His glances made my knees weak, and I had to be careful not to stumble.

"And people come all the way from the big city to sleep in log cabins? In the middle of nowhere?" John asked skeptically.

"Yes. Believe me, if there's one thing I missed in the big city, it's space for intimacy," I answered. But what I really meant was a place to be alone, because I hadn't let anyone get close to me in the big city.

John came towards me and only stopped when his masculine scent of cedarwood enveloped me.

"Do you have someone in the big city with whom you wish for intimacy?"

His voice was rough and hoarse. He was the big bad wolf, and I was the little girl who had walked right into his trap.

I shook my head. What a silly question! The place in my heart was reserved for him, and no other man had ever found room there.

"No one?" John asked again.

"No one. It's always been you," I answered softly.

John smiled with satisfaction, his eyes glinting darkly.

"You're the only one I've ever wanted, and I still lay claim to you."

My lower abdomen clenched, and goosebumps crawled up my back. John was touching me with his gaze, and he knew it.

He grabbed me by the shoulders, exactly like yesterday, and then he kissed me. This time, I didn't think of resisting or running away. The moment was far too beautiful for that. With each kiss, John put another piece of my broken heart back together.

"I'm not letting you go again," John murmured.

"Is that a threat?" I asked hoarsely.

"No, a promise!"

John pushed me against the nearest tree before kissing me again. His soft lips tasted sweet, and his rough stubble tickled my cheeks. He growled softly and deeply, and I fell in love with that sound.

"It's dangerous," I sighed, while my hands, as if of their own accord, unbuttoned his blue shirt and stroked over his defined muscles.

"What?" John asked, although we both knew what I meant. But John wanted me to face the danger head-on.

"This, what we're doing."

He smiled at me. "Trust me, suppressing it is even more dangerous. I can't resist you any longer."

And I couldn't resist him any longer, I never could. So I remained silent in agreement, tilted my head back, and enjoyed the feelings John was stirring in me. He took off his cowboy hat and placed it on my head. The scent of leather and John clouded my senses.

John knelt before me, pushed my dress up, and with a quick movement, pulled my panties down.

"Not here," I moaned, while my body offered no resistance.

"Yes, right here," John murmured, his eyes flashing darkly at me.

It felt so forbidden that it excited me even more to let it happen.

With his hands, John reached around me and massaged my butt. I was trapped in his grip and loved being his prey.

"Your sweet ass drove me crazy yesterday," John growled.

"I know," I answered, smiling with satisfaction.

Of course, I had known that my black dress would fly up at full gallop, and the thrill of the forbidden had tempted me to do nothing about it.

When John kissed my shaved mound, he murmured softly, and a tremor went through my body. His gentle kisses moved further down until he reached my clit. His warm breath alone was enough to make me moan. With his tongue, he parted my labia and massaged me with circular movements, bringing me closer and closer to orgasm.

His tongue felt so good, my whole body trembled with desire. With one hand, I clutched John's thick hair, with the other, I held onto the tree trunk.

I was ready for him and I wanted to feel him inside me at last.

"Please, take me," I moaned. But John just smiled at me while continuing to lick my sensitive pearl.

"Please," I begged once more, close to orgasm. I wanted to come together with John, so I held back my orgasm as best I could.

I was more than ready for him, I could feel the wetness between my trembling legs.

When he entered me with two fingers, I moaned loudly.

"John!" I cried out, just before I came.

"Come for me, baby," he murmured.

"No," I protested.

"Come for me," John commanded dominantly.

His fingers massaging my most sensitive spot, his tongue on my pearl, and his dominant gaze practically forced me to orgasm.

And what a gigantic orgasm it was! Truly, I had never come so intensely before.

But John didn't give me a breather. He stood up, opened his pants, grabbed me by the thighs, and entered me while I was pressed between his strong body and the tree.

"Next time, you'll come for me when I command you to!" John growled.

"Or else you'll spank me?" I asked jokingly. There was no question that there would be a next time, because John's attraction was too strong for me to resist.

"Yes," John answered seriously, and my cheeks reddened. Why did I want to find out how serious John really was about his answer? And why did I love that dominant look so much?

John thrust deep into me. So deep that I felt too full and at the same time wanted more. His rough cheeks rubbed against my neck and his hot breath whispered over my skin. A salty film of sweat formed on his bare chest, glistening in the sun. His muscles tensed with the rhythm of his thrusts, and I was sure that John trained even more for his perfect body than he used to.

"Don't let me run away again," I sighed softly.

"Damn," John panted. "Never."

Every single word we spoke came directly from our hearts. We showed our feelings without fear or pride, while John fucked the soul out of my body.

I felt John's erection grow even harder... and harder!

"Come for me," John gasped, and this time I didn't resist him.

I came, wrapping my legs even tighter around John's hips. The second orgasm was even more intense than the first, and I soared on the waves into other realms.

John thrust hard a few more times, then he came too, pumping his gold into me.

Chapter 8 – John

"I really missed this view," June sighed, and I knew exactly what she meant.

I played with the loose ends of the reins hanging from Copper's bridle while my gaze swept over the morning mist.

"Understandable, no one could drive me out of paradise either," I said. It was true, I loved *Red Rivers* and all of Merryville, but paradise only existed in combination with June.

"It's incredible that everything still looks exactly the same as back then," June noted, and I nodded.

Yet everything had changed. When June left, everything seemed gray and desolate, empty and lonely. Since June had returned, she had brought sunshine back into my life, even if the situation between us was strange.

We had only been building the vacation ranch for a few days, and there was a hell of a lot to do, but already the thought of June leaving again once everything was built was driving me crazy. June couldn't leave. I wouldn't allow it. Not again.

Since our liaison, her fearful heart and my bruised pride had decided never to talk about it. We both pretended it was *just sex*, nothing more, although neither of us believed this lie. There was more between us than just a good fuck.

Of course, every time I saw her perky ass or her breasts, I wanted to fuck June in every conceivable position, but it was more than that.

Every time she smiled, I wanted to take her in my arms and protect her so that her smile would never fade.

And every time I looked at June like that, she returned my gaze and longed for my arms.

"How about a race?" June asked challengingly.

My gaze switched back and forth between June and Champion. Although they had been separated for years, it hadn't taken a day for the two to harmonize perfectly again.

Poor Champ. It would hit him even harder when June went back to New York.

"Afraid of losing?" June asked again. She patted Champ's caramel-colored coat, which shimmered golden in the morning sun.

I cleared my throat and pushed my thoughts aside. "No, I was just thinking about what I should get when I win."

"No chance, so you don't have to rack your brains about it," June replied confidently.

"I really should spank your ass," I muttered.

June immediately became embarrassed, and her cheeks reddened. Damn, those big green eyes were driving me crazy. June and I, we belonged together. Period. End of story.

I just had to convince her of that.

... and that she would enjoy a red-hot bottom more than she thought.

"Scared?" I asked, grinning three times as confidently as June had earlier.

"You're dreaming," she answered with a hot voice.

"Good. If I win, I'll spank your ass. And if you win..."

"Then I never want to hear about red bottoms again," June replied curtly.

"Fine by me," I said. Then we got our horses ready, nodded, and galloped off. I let June and Champion pass me while I held Copper back, which he didn't like at all.

"Easy, buddy," I reassured my horse. "We'll still win, don't panic."

I had ridden Champ for years and knew he was a damn good horse when it came to roping. As long as he had something to chase, he gave it his all. But if I stayed behind him long enough, Champ would get bored faster than June could say *Ouch*, and I would use that to my advantage and race past him with Copper.

Not to mention I could ogle June's shapely behind. The skin-tight jeans she was wearing had been turning my head all morning. She also wore a plaid shirt that she had tied above her navel.

Now she looked like the beautiful cowgirl from the old days again, only a hat was missing.

Confidently, June threw a glance over her shoulder at me as she galloped along the south pasture towards *Farley Ranch*.

But just before the border fence, I let Copper's reins loose, and he raced past June at full hunting gallop. Behind the finish line, I didn't need to say anything more; a simple grin was enough to bring the blush of shame to her face.

"I'll come back to that when I'm in the mood for it," I murmured. Then I dismounted and led Copper into the paddock. The round, fenced-in area and the barn were the only buildings still standing.

Unfortunately, the second architect had the same sobering view as his predecessor, which is why June's grandparents' house had been demolished the day before yesterday. All the furniture was now in the barn. Tim, my uncle, had spent all of yesterday transporting the construction debris away, while I had tried to distract June. She was holding up bravely, but I knew exactly how much the sight had hurt her. She had grown up in that house. If someone were to tear down *Red Rivers*, I'd be just as devastated.

June followed me silently into the paddock, unsaddled Champ, and placed the saddle on the fence.

"What's next?" I asked, clapping my hands. I was the man for the rough work; I left the organization to June, Sophia, and Elli. Though my youngest sister had her hands full with Citizen Silver.

"We're laying out the floor plans for the vacation homes," June said. She pressed various papers into my hand, on which different drawings were displayed.

"That's quite a lot of designs."

June nodded. "I know. But each cabin gets its own charm and therefore a different layout." Her eyes sparkled as she talked about how she wanted to breathe life into the individual houses.

Damn, New York could really be glad to have June. She must be doing a hell of a good job.

We staked out the layouts of the wooden cabins one after another, ten in total, and surveyed our work.

"This is perfect," June gushed.

"Damn right. Your city friends will love it. I already know which cabin I'll be spanking your sweet ass in."

"John!" June spluttered in shock. "In none of the houses!"

I loved throwing June off balance and hoped I'd have plenty more opportunities to do so. Admittedly, since June had been living in the guesthouse, I'd been trying to spend every free minute with her, because she'd run away from me for long enough. June belonged to me, and now I was staking my claim on her.

"Trust me, you'll love it," I murmured. June would love it, she just didn't know it yet.

"But not in our paradise vacation cabins." She put her hands on her hips and looked at me seriously. I returned her gaze calmly.

"You'll love it everywhere."

June didn't say anything more now, just stared at me with her mouth open. I took her chin between my thumb and forefinger and kissed her gently but firmly.

"I'll show you a few more things you'll love."

"Oh really?" June asked timidly.

"Yes."

She bit her lower lip thoughtfully, having no idea how seductive she looked doing it. June had no idea how much power she really had over me. I would kill for a single one of her glances, travel to the end of the world for a brief laugh, move heaven and earth for a kiss.

I almost grabbed June by the shoulders, pushed her to the ground, and shoved my hard cock into her mouth, but I managed to stop myself when I saw the dust clouds on the horizon.

June looked at her silver watch and gazed at me questioningly. "Actually, Sophia wasn't planning to bring in the heavy artillery until the afternoon because she still has to make a few phone calls."

"Hm." I stuck my hands in my pockets and growled. Whoever was coming had better have a good excuse for ruining my blowjob.

When I saw Rachel's signal-red Ferrari, I glanced at June, who was glaring daggers at the car.

"She must have just taken a wrong turn," I said with a shrug.

"Definitely. Hell is in the other direction."

I grinned as I wiped the sweat from my forehead. Hell couldn't be much hotter than this damn midsummer heat.

"That wasn't a joke," June said seriously when she saw my grin.

"Be nice," I replied as the car drew closer.

June snorted indignantly before taking a deep breath and sighing.

"I know as well as you do how desperately we need her money. To be honest, even with all my savings, it's going to be pretty tight."

"I know."

Damn heat!

It was destroying our crops and thus our livelihood, and it was also fogging up my brain. I couldn't think straight during the day anymore. A small part of me blamed not the heat, but June for my inability to think.

"Do you know what she wants here?" June asked.

"No idea," I answered.

"She certainly doesn't want to see me. I'll go ahead and get the horses ready so we can ride back. I need an ice-cold shower."

"Sounds good."

I leaned against the paddock and watched June as she groomed the horses while Rachel got out of the car. Her face was once again hidden behind huge black sunglasses.

"Yoo-hoo!" Rachel called out and waved to us. I nodded to her and went to meet her. Mainly to cut short her unannounced visit, if possible. That's why I got straight to the point.

"What brings you here, Rachel?"

"I wanted to see how you're progressing," Rachel answered innocently and ran her fingers through her loose blonde hair.

"Good," I said curtly. Then I wondered how Rachel even knew what we were doing. Before I could ask, Rachel laughed loudly.

"Oh, Elli told me about the project."

"Ah."

Rachel walked around the property with interest, as if she owned it. Of course. She was a Pearson, and a Pearson could potentially own anything that could be bought with money.

"The main house is gone," Rachel observed, removing her sunglasses with a grand gesture. "I would have done the same. The house was already showing its age years ago." Rachel spoke so loudly that June must have heard her. I glanced at her, but she continued to focus on grooming the horses.

"The house had a soul," I replied. But what would a soulless being like Rachel understand about a soul?

Damn, only now did I fully realize how much I had hurt June back then.

"Maybe. Whatever. There's still a lot to do, can you two really handle it alone?"

I didn't answer, just looked at Rachel seriously.

"And what's going to happen with those staked-out things? Flower beds?" she asked quickly when she saw my unmistakable look.

"Vacation homes," I growled. It took all my self-control not to yell at Rachel. That's why I had even more respect for June, because she didn't let it show at all. She calmly saddled Champion and then scratched his favorite spot between his ears.

"Cute," Rachel replied haughtily. Either she was trying to provoke June into attacking her, or she was even more lacking in empathy than I had thought.

"Why are you here?" I asked.

"Actually, I'm here because of our summer festival."

I raised an eyebrow questioningly. "Because of the summer festival?"

"Yes. You need to do me a small favor."

"Oh, do I?" I hated it when someone barked orders at me.

"Just a tiny little favor." Rachel held her thumb and index finger close together. "We've decided to increase the prize money for each competition to five thousand dollars, but the posters have already been printed. And since you volunteer at the fire department and have good connections..."

"You want me to play messenger and let everyone know?"

"Exactly! That would be great." Rachel clapped her hands.

"Fine, whatever."

"I hope you'll also participate in one or two events. Wild, unpredictable broncs await you," Rachel winked at me, then got back into her sports car and sped away.

Damn, it was hard enough to convince June to stay without Rachel, but with Rachel, it became almost impossible. I could feel June's jealous glances behind me, and I hated Rachel for it.

A single, stupid kiss between Rachel and me - for which I wasn't to blame, mind you - and everything was ruined. But this time it would be different, even if I had to keep Rachel away from me with an electric cattle prod.

I went back to June and the horses, which were ready for the ride back. June was already sitting on Champ, leaning on the horn of her western saddle.

"What did she want? After her scathing criticism of our project, I haven't heard anything else."

"The prize money for the competitions at the summer festival has been increased to five thousand dollars. Apart from that, Rachel has no idea, okay?"

Even though June tried to appear disinterested, I could see the pain in her eyes.

"What if she's right? What if our project fails? What if we don't have enough money and I've caused you even more problems?"

"Since when do you take life advice from Rachel Pearson?" I asked cynically.

"Since she raised valid doubts. What if we can't handle all of this?"

I placed my hand on June's thigh. "Why do you always let Rachel get into your head? Just ignore her, like we all do."

"Oh, so I just imagined that kiss between you two back then?"

I should have known June would misunderstand.

"June," I began. But June slapped my hand off her thigh and spurred Champion on.

"No, June. Stop running away all the damn time!" I snapped at her and grabbed Champ's reins. I forced her horse to a stop, which didn't bother June further. She jumped out of the saddle and ran past me.

Without thinking, I swung myself into the saddle, spurred Champion on, and grabbed a lasso that was hanging on one of the fence posts.

"Sorry buddy, I'll be right back," I said to Copper, who was impatiently pawing the ground in the paddock.

Then I let Champ trot loosely, swung the lasso, and gained momentum. When June saw what I was about to do, she gasped loudly.

"Don't you dare catch me with a lasso! I'm not a cow!"

"Then stop running away from me and your problems!" I yelled back and gave June one last chance to stop.

She kept running. It took exactly two more seconds for the loop of the lasso to wrap around her upper body. Although June was now standing still, I pulled the lasso taut.

"I warned you," I said, unable to suppress a grin.

"John!" June snapped at me. "Let me go!"

"Not with that tone, madam." I pulled the rope a little tighter.

June glared at me with death stares but remained silent.

"Good girl," I praised her.

June snorted contemptuously. "You'd like that, wouldn't you."

I loved her resistance. But I had the upper hand. June couldn't run away from me anymore.

Then I dismounted Champ and walked once around June. "Aren't you tired of constantly running away?"

"Yes," June sighed.

"Good. Then stop doing it."

"It's not as simple as you think." I saw pain and uncertainty in her face, reflected in her shining emerald eyes. With my thumb, I wiped away a tear that rolled down her cheek.

"Life is never simple. But there are people who help us bear everything. I can help you, you just have to let me."

"And how?"

"By trusting me."

"That's not as simple as you think either." June sighed.

"I know," I murmured. "Do you still love me?"

June looked at me, confused. She didn't know what to say, although we both knew how she felt. Of course she still loved me, just as I still loved her. Neither thousands of miles nor years without contact had changed that.

"I still love you," June whispered, which elicited a satisfied smile from me.

"Then you owe it to both of us to give me a chance," I said, and June nodded.

I took her chin between my thumb and forefinger, and we sealed our pact with a kiss. Her soft, full lips tasted like honey.

"I never had a chance to resist you," June whispered.

"Neither did I," I murmured.

If that wasn't a sign from heaven. We couldn't keep our hands off each other, no matter how much we fought against it. But now we didn't have to fight anymore.

June was mine. Period.

"Do you want to untie me now?" June asked, shrugging her shoulders.

"No," I answered with a smile. "I'm not going to risk you running away from me again."

"So you want to keep me tied up forever?" June asked, amused.

"I'd love to, yes," I answered seriously. The smile disappeared from June's face... and was then replaced by a seductive grin.

"Would you like that?" I asked.

"Maybe," June purred dreamily, while her eyes screamed *Yes*.

I would like it too, my beauty.

"On your knees," I commanded, as I unbuttoned my jeans.

"Now? Here?" June looked at me with big, round eyes and a questioning face.

"Now. Here."

June let her gaze wander over the vast property. We were standing on the south pasture of *Red Rivers*, about a hundred meters from the former main house of the *Farley Ranch*.

"What if someone sees us? People are coming and going all the time right now," June sighed. Unconsciously, she licked her lips. I smiled as I rubbed the bulge in my pants.

Her soft, trembling voice was music to my ears. She sounded so innocent, so sweet, and yet I knew exactly that June craved the thrill of the forbidden just as much as I did.

June was right, people were constantly coming to load or unload something, and theoretically, anyone could see us.

"Then you'd better hurry before someone shows up."

I opened my pants completely, and my hard cock sprang out. June alternated between staring at my face and my erection. Moaning softly, June got on her knees and opened her mouth.

Her open mouth was an invitation I didn't refuse. I moved closer and June licked my erection with her tongue.

"Look at me while you do it," I groaned.

June obeyed me as she licked my tip more and more greedily.

She was hungry. Damn hungry. And I had exactly what she needed to satisfy her hunger.

I took another step closer to her and thrust my cock into her throat.

Warm. Tight. Wet.

The look June gave me was absolutely delicious. Finally, I was getting my damn blowjob.

June's soft lips closed tightly around my hard cock, and I moaned in relief as I entered her mouth. Her tongue played around my tip and then traveled along my shaft. Again and again, June enveloped my hardness and sucked on it with pleasure, while moaning sensually.

Had she always been this naughty? In any case, there was no doubt that she enjoyed our decadent game. Just the thought of being caught made my cock even harder. I stroked June's full, brown hair and buried my hands in it before roughly pulling it to thrust even deeper into her.

June moaned with pleasure. In her emerald eyes burned a fire that screamed for more.

More! Harder! Deeper!

There were moments when I wanted to carry June on my hands, like a gentleman.

And there were moments when I just wanted to thrust damn deep into her, not like a gentleman.

As it looked, June extraordinarily enjoyed that I was now taking what I wanted. She tilted her head back so I could penetrate even deeper into her throat until I buried my cock to the hilt in her.

"You make me so damn horny, baby," I gasped.

June answered with looks because my hardness didn't give her time to speak. Usually, I reined in my dominance like a wild mustang, but with June, I didn't have to restrain myself. June could handle me, and her looks were clear - during the day she wanted the gentleman and at night the beast. And sometimes also in the late morning.

Now June sucked harder on my tip and I gasped loudly while she moaned sensually. Louder and louder. Damn, everyone within three miles could hear us.

Good! Then everyone would hear that June belonged to me alone.

I wanted to come inside her, keep fucking her, and come again. What June was doing with her mouth and tongue was perfect. After sunset, June was no sweet angel anymore, but my whore.

"You belong to me," I growled as I continued to fuck her mouth. "Only to me, and that's been true since I first saw you."

My lasso was still wrapped around June's shoulders and upper arms, but that didn't stop her from touching herself. I thrust into her harder and harder, deeper and deeper, and I loved how June moaned and brought herself closer and closer to orgasm.

Damn, June was driving me crazy. Breathing heavily, moaning, trembling with lust, with my cock between her full lips. This sight burned itself into my memory, yet I wanted to repeat our love affair in the open field soon, the view simply pleased me too much. With more rope and less clothing.

"Come for me, baby," I murmured in a husky voice. I watched June as her orgasm approached. Her green eyes shimmered, and the flames consuming us were further stoked by the sparks between us.

She came, and satisfied, I concentrated on my own orgasm, which wasn't far behind. I enjoyed a few final, deep thrusts, and then I released, breathing heavily, into her mouth.

June's soft lips remained tightly closed around my cock until I came back to my senses, then I brushed a strand of her silky brown hair from her face.

"You can be a good girl after all," I murmured. "You should try it more often. The good girl look suits you."

"You'll have to convince me of that," June replied with a challenging look.

"Is that a threat?" I asked.

"No, a promise."

Chapter 9 – June

I leaned against the wooden fence framing the large sand arena, watching Elli work with Rachel's super expensive and beautiful show jumper. We had set up the obstacles together, which Citizen Silver cleared with flying colors, without touching a single pole.

"Fantastic!" I cheered them on, and Elli brought the show jumper to a halt in front of me, bowing from the saddle as if I were a judge.

"Would you mind raising the jumps a bit?" Elli asked, smiling at me shyly. Although I often offered her my help, Elli was frequently hesitant to accept it.

"Sure, no problem," I replied, climbing over the fence and raising one obstacle after another.

When I wasn't busy with construction work on the Farley Ranch or having my brains fucked out by John, I watched Elli work with the horses. John hadn't exaggerated when he said she had a gift.

"Man, these are really high," I said in awe. The top rail of the obstacles was at my eye level.

"Citizen Silver will get us over safely," Elli replied confidently. Then she clicked her tongue and galloped a large circle around the arena before jumping the obstacles—no, flying over them! One after another, as if they were nothing.

"That was incredible," I blurted out. "Hard to believe he wouldn't even lift a hoof not too long ago."

"He was just bored. A few rides here, a little cuddling there, and boom, everything's back on track." Elli bashfully brushed a curl from her face.

"You shouldn't downplay your work like that. Without you, Citizen Silver would still be refusing to even look at obstacles."

Although Elli was the spitting image of Sophia and their grandmother—with the loosest mouth in the world—she was much shyer than the rest of the Keys.

"Calling it a day," Elli said, jumping out of the saddle and leading Citizen Silver off the arena.

"I wish I could call it a day too," I sighed, tilting my head back.

"Is there still a lot to do?" Elli asked, and I nodded.

There was an endless amount to do! The vacation homes were all standing, but windows and doors still needed to be installed. And the electricity only worked intermittently so far. The biggest problem was that we were slowly but surely running out of money because new, unforeseen issues kept cropping up. Problems I never faced in New York.

"Can I help somehow?"

"Keep Rachel off our backs," I answered cynically.

Since Rachel's horse was here, Rachel practically was too, and we all knew it wasn't about Citizen Silver.

"Alright, next time I'll grab a crucifix and holy water from Gram's drawer," Elli giggled, and I laughed along.

As we walked past Champion, who was standing in his stall munching on hay, I stopped. His head immediately shot up, and he came over for some petting.

"John told me you used to compete with Champ."

"Yeah, that's right."

"How was he?" I asked curiously.

Elli stopped. "Are you asking for a specific reason?"

"No," I lied. Of course, I was asking for a very specific reason.

"It's about the prize money at the Pearsons' annual summer festival, isn't it?"

"Busted. But don't tell anyone. It was just a thought."

"My lips are sealed," Elli promised and closed her mouth with an imaginary key. "What do you want to do with the prize money? Five thousand dollars is a lot of money."

I nodded and sighed heavily. "The windows for the last five apartments will only be delivered if we can pay cash upfront. I could explain a rustic vacation rental without beds to the city folks, but a house without windows? Not so much."

My finances were depleted. Thanks to Sophia's skills, we managed to negotiate prices or delay bills, but the vacation ranch cost twice as much as initially thought.

"What? Do city folks know that windows exist in the countryside?" Elli chuckled.

I laughed briefly before becoming serious again.

"Yeah. But before I can spend the prize money on windows, I need to win. It's been years since I last competed in a tournament, and for Champ too. So, how was he?" I asked a second time.

"He was good," Elli answered briefly, and I expected a *but*, yet none came. Elli looked me up and down, and I knew she wanted to protect my feelings.

"John told me you eventually quit because he stopped winning ribbons. What happened?"

Elli led Citizen Silver into his stall and removed his saddle while talking to me.

"Champ was good, but unhappy. He didn't enjoy the competitions."

"What?" I asked in surprise. "If anyone loves the hustle, the music, and the excitement in the air, it's Champ."

Elli shrugged. "Not the Champ I rode."

"We've all really changed," I whispered softly. But were changes always bad? Wasn't change less scary than being stuck in the status quo forever? My heart would have preferred to maintain the status quo, with John, Champ, and Merryville, but my head would always run away from the past.

Elli leaned conspiratorially over Citizen Silver's stall door and tapped out her curry comb.

"Should I train you and Champ?"

I laughed out loud. "You're really good at what you do, but you can't work miracles." As I finished my thought, I became more serious. "And if what you're saying is true, and Champ has lost his joy for competitions, we shouldn't even try."

Elli looked at me earnestly, and suddenly she didn't seem like a teenager anymore, but like a very wise woman who knew what she was talking about. "Champion won those ribbons for you, not for anyone else. He wants to make you proud, have fun with you, stand in the spotlight with you."

"Do you really think so?"

"Yep. You can trust me on this. John says I'm the best in the field."

I smiled. "Well, if John says so, it must be true."

"He talks a lot of nonsense, but that's true. And he still loves you. I don't know if he's told you yet, but that's true too."

My laughter choked off. "How do you know that?" I asked hoarsely.

"Because it's obvious that you both still love each other."

I didn't know how to respond to that, so I kept quiet. John and I, mainly me, wanted to keep our liaison a secret for now. I should've been indifferent to what others thought, but I wasn't. Everyone here knew about the drama from back then, and this time I didn't want to be remembered as little June Farley who fled to New York with a broken heart - again.

"Would you really train me?" I asked. I knew I should have said something about John's and my relationship, but I couldn't bring myself to do it.

"Of course. We could train you at the pasture west of the river, it's quiet there."

"That would be great."

"By when do you need to get on the list?"

I thought for a moment. "By the day after tomorrow. The cutting competition is first thing on Saturday."

"How exciting! You and Champ are going to clean up!"

While Elli continued to take care of Citizen Silver, I went to the feed room to prepare the feed. As I did so, I cast a furtive glance at Nougat's box, because the goat that had suddenly appeared in one of the pastures liked to go on adventures. When I saw the empty box, I wasn't really surprised. Because we always found her somewhere on the farm, no one worried too much about the goat's safety.

"Nougat's gone on an adventure," I said with a sigh.

"She's probably in the hay storage again. I'll check on her in a bit."

"Okay," I said and continued to prepare the feed.

The roar of a sports car made all the horses' heads in the stable perk up, and I sighed.

"Speak of the devil."

Elli patted Citizen Silver's coat, then left the box.

"I guess I'll go get Gram's Exorcism-for-Beginners kit from the drawer."

"Absolutely not," I said seriously and grabbed Elli's upper arm. "You're staying with me."

Rachel got out of her fire-red Ferrari, threw a furry bag over her shoulder and strutted towards us.

"Heyyy," she greeted us in a drawn-out tone. "How's it going with you?"

"Great. I think you can take Citizen Silver back tomorrow," Elli said, while I remained silent. Just one more day, and I wouldn't have to endure Rachel anymore. I hated that she was meddling in my life and my relationships again, as it suited her.

"Oh," Rachel replied, surprised. Almost as if she regretted that her horse was healthy.

"Yep. He's back to his old self."

"Great," Rachel said. Her voice was a pitch too high to sound credible. Then there was silence. Silence and death glares that Rachel and I exchanged silently, while poor Elli stood in the line of fire.

I knew it was childish, but I didn't trust Rachel one bit. She was planning something, and I would watch her like a hawk. She wouldn't destroy my dreams again.

Not today. Not tomorrow. Never again!

"Say, Rachel. Do you have the participant list for the tournaments at the summer festival with you?" I asked, putting on my most beautiful smile.

"Of course, always. I want to stay up to date," she gasped. Rachel pulled a clipboard out of her fluffy fur bag that looked like an exploded raccoon.

"Is there still a spot on the list for the cutting competition?"

"Oh, I'm sorry my dear, unfortunately not." She pouted, and I concentrated on not jumping in her face. She wasn't sorry about anything. Besides, I was sure there were still free spots. At not a single tournament the Pearsons organized were the lists so full that they didn't accept anyone else.

I looked at Elli, shrugged my shoulders and pretended I didn't care that I was excluded from the tournament. "Well, then I'll have more time for the vacation homes."

Elli winked at me. "We'll train anyway. The next tournament will come soon enough."

"Definitely," Rachel said with the fakest smile in the world.

"By the way, John is at the Farley Ranch. I think he and Tim are still laying the floors," Elli said. She voiced what we both thought. Rachel didn't come a single time because of Citizen Silver, only because of John.

Rachel ran her hand through her shoulder-length blonde hair and grinned at us.

"I'm not here because of John, but because of you." Rachel pointed her index finger like a gun at Elli.

"Because of me?" Elli asked surprised and turned to the horse box behind her. "Or Citizen Silver?"

"Yes, because of you. There are two more horses you should work with."

My jaw dropped. Elli looked just as surprised.

"Two more horses?"

"Yes. Of course, I'll pay in advance again. And for the good work with Citizen Silver, there's an extra check."

"Well, I don't know," Elli sighed. She looked at me sympathetically, and I shook my head. I loved her for wanting to turn down the job offer, but I knew about the debts that had piled up at *Red Rivers*, and it would be a while before the holiday ranch turned a profit.

"I'll pay double," Rachel offered.

Elli gave me another look to make sure I was certain. And I was. For the Keys, I would put my pride aside and endure Rachel for a few more weeks.

"Okay. I'll take a look at the two of them. You can bring them tomorrow."

"Great! Then I'll come by with them tomorrow," Rachel cheered and clapped her hands enthusiastically. "I'll be off then."

Elli raised her hand. "Wait, I have one more question."

"Hm?" Rachel asked, tilting her head.

"Is there still a spot open in the team roping?"

"Team roping?" Rachel asked curiously.

"Yes." Elli led Rachel to a white horse standing in its stall. I wondered why Elli was telling her all this. She kept winking at me, but I had no idea what she was up to.

"This is Phoenix, and I've been working with him for weeks. He used to be afraid of cows."

Rachel burst out laughing. "A ranch horse afraid of cows?"

"He's not anymore. And I'd like to put Phoenix through a tough test."

Rachel looked at her clipboard. "You're in luck, there's still one spot left."

"Sold!" Elli said excitedly.

"Who should I put on the participant list? You and Sophia?"

Elli shook her head and grinned widely. "June Farley and John Key."

My heart skipped a beat.

I gave Elli a look that said: *Are you crazy? John hates roping!*

Elli looked at me smiling, and her eyes answered: *Don't panic, we'll manage this.*

And Rachel's looks? Well, if looks could kill, we'd both be dead.

While Rachel continued to glare at me, Elli looked at me grinning. "Come on, let's go find Nougat."

I nodded, even though I would have liked to bask in Rachel's envious glares a little longer.

Chapter 10 – John

I need to talk to you.

A sentence nobody likes to hear, because it always spells trouble. Without exception. What storm was waiting for me, I still didn't know, because I hadn't seen June since that fateful sentence. By now, dusk was falling.

I paced back and forth relentlessly in front of the veranda of the first nearly finished vacation cabin. Last night, Tom and I had finished laying the floor. After I'd dragged the heavy wooden furniture inside, June and Sophia had locked themselves in to decorate. That was hours ago, and June hadn't shown her face once. I was about to explode, even though I tried to remain calm. I'd kept myself busy with minor handyman jobs on the other houses.

We were in a financial tight spot, which brought our project to a standstill so close to the finish line.

"John!" Sophia called out and waved to me as they finally came out of the godforsaken vacation house. June waved too, but avoided making eye contact. What was on her mind? Was she going back to New York or had she done something? The uncertainty was driving me absolutely crazy.

I walked towards them.

"So? Finished?" I asked.

"Finished and absolutely dreamy!" Sophia gushed. She waved the digital camera around. "I'll upload the photos to the website right away. Anyone who sees them will immediately fall in love with this cabin. And I promise you, I'll shove them under everyone's nose."

"Sounds good," I grumbled. "Will you show me what I've been slaving away for weeks?"

I looked at June seriously, signaling that I wanted an answer from her.

"Of course. Come with me," she said shyly.

"Have fun, you two. I've got to go now," Sophia said goodbye.

"Where do you need to go?" June asked uncertainly.

Damn it, what was wrong with her? Did she want to tell me what she wanted to say while my little sister was present? Why?

"Um," Sophia began to speak, as if she didn't quite know what she wanted to say. "I have to go because..." Sophia held the camera close to her heart while frantically searching for an excuse.

"Because you need to upload the pictures?" I helped her out.

"Yes, exactly! The pictures should be online today! So, see you later. Or tomorrow."

Sophia got into my truck, stalled the engine twice in her excitement, and then roared off while we silently watched her leave.

"You're so quiet," I murmured.

June flinched as if I'd caught her doing something indecent. "Not at all."

"Yes, you are. Ever since you said you wanted to talk to me about something."

"Oh, it's not that important. We'll talk about it later."

She shrugged, took my hand, and wordlessly led me to the first, completely finished vacation house.

Later? Damn, I was half crazy imagining horror scenarios!

I stopped, grabbed June's wrist, and pulled her swiftly towards me. Her emerald green eyes sparkled at me, and I forced her to hold my gaze.

"June. Tell me what's going on."

"Nothing. Really."

"Then why are you acting so strange? Do you want to leave again?"

With that, I had spoken the unspeakable. If June was going to rip my heart out of my chest again, I at least wanted to know beforehand so I could brace myself for the pain.

"What? No!" June snorted. "What makes you think that?"

"Because of your damn secrecy. You can hardly look me in the eye."

After I said it, June looked me straight in the eye. Damn, the most beautiful woman in the world was standing in front of me, holding my heart in her hand. It was entirely up to her whether she protected it or crushed it right now with her bare fingers.

"June, tell me what's going on," I said in a more conciliatory tone.

"It was a stupid idea. Please don't hate me for it," June whispered.

"What stupid idea should I hate you for?"

"Elli and I signed you up for team roping."

"You did what?" I asked in disbelief. I had expected anything else, horrific news that would shred my heart, collapse my worldview, and drive me to alcoholism. But this?

I burst out laughing and hugged June.

"I would never hate you for something like that."

More than that, I was sure I wasn't capable of hating June. She had dragged my heart to New York and I didn't hate her.

"Why are you laughing? I thought you hated roping? And competitions like that?" June asked, astonished.

"I do," I grumbled. "But judging by your looks, I was expecting far worse."

"So you'll compete with me in team roping?" June asked, surprised.

"Better take Elli, she's the horse expert," I said. I hadn't competed since my accident with that damn hellish bronc. And certainly not in roping.

"Elli is the horse expert, true. And you're the better cowboy."

"Come on, what do we have to lose? Best case scenario, we win money that we desperately need. And worst case, Champ and I will embarrass ourselves because we're both out of shape."

"Maybe you, but certainly not Champion," I said and immediately regretted it.

"What do you mean by that?"

I didn't really want to rub it in anyone's face that Champ and I had been secretly swinging the lasso to be a little closer to June.

"Never mind. We'll talk about it another time. Now show me the cabin already. I want to see if you're really as talented as all of New York claims."

"An entire city?" June asked, amused, and giggled.

"The internet doesn't lie," I replied, grinning, and her smile disappeared.

"But it doesn't always tell the truth either," June sighed.

We entered the finished vacation house and damn, New York and the entire internet had understated it. June was a goddess of interior design. Even I, a simple country cowboy, was blown away by the decor.

The wooden bed with the faux fur runner and white curtains, resembling a canopy bed, was illuminated by string lights. Candles stood on the old wooden nightstands that June had taken from the main house. Logs were already placed in the fireplace, and I wanted nothing more than to lock myself in here with June forever.

"Well? What do you think?"

"Perfect. It feels like *home*," I answered.

"That's exactly the reaction I was hoping for," June whispered.

I gently kissed her forehead before taking another tour through the small log cabin.

"But one thing's missing," I stated matter-of-factly.

"Really? What?" June asked, puzzled. Her eyes darted nervously around the room, searching for a flaw.

"I can't tie you up anywhere."

"Oh," June sighed softly, her cheeks turning red. I gripped her upper arms and gazed deeply into her beautiful emerald eyes.

"How else am I supposed to prevent my beauty from running away again?"

"You could simply ask her if she'll stay."

I smiled contentedly, closed the door, and drew the blackout curtains.

"Then be a good girl and undress," I murmured.

June obeyed and let her clothes fall to the floor in front of me. At first, June had protested, not wanting to admit how devious we both were. Over time, though, June was able to drop this facade, which led to even more fun.

Damn, she turned me on in the most absurd places, in the craziest situations - and she felt the same way.

The soft candlelight reflected off her smooth, flawless skin, tanned by the Texan summer sun.

She smiled. Damn, I loved that seductive smile on her full, curved lips that tasted like honey. I kissed her and gently nibbled on her lower lip, making June moan.

"Say you won't run away," I commanded.

"I won't run away," June whispered. Her voice trembled with arousal, just like her body.

"Lie down and prove it to me." My own voice was foreign to me, sounding so rough and husky. But when I saw June in front of me, naked, my animal instincts took over and I took what I wanted.

I grabbed June's hips and lifted her onto the bed as light as a feather. She ran her fingers through her silky brown hair and smiled seductively at me. Her sensual appearance drove me crazy, and I almost forgot my manners. But only almost. A gentleman savors.

I leaned forward to kiss her honey-sweet lips. My kisses trailed down her cheek to her neck, over her collarbone to her womanly breasts. Her buds were hard and grew even harder as I licked over them. June writhed blissfully under my kisses and sighed. With my tongue, I traveled over her body, wanting to taste her everywhere. Her flavor would still linger on my tongue long after I'd fucked her.

"Hold still," I growled. Then I took one of the candles from the nightstand and dripped candle wax onto her stomach.

"Oh God," June moaned loudly as her stomach tensed. I loved how June squirmed, but I loved her facial expression even more when she fought against her instincts to obey me.

Another hot drop touched her skin above her navel. This time June held still. More and more candle wax dripped onto her flawless body, covering her skin. On her stomach, her sides, her collarbone, her arms. The gentleman in me gave June time to get used to the wax on her skin. The beast in me circled the candle around her breasts, and the distance to her nipples grew smaller and smaller.

"Oh God," June gasped again. Her body trembled with lust. Her hands yearned for my muscular body, and her center yearned for my cock.

"Leave God out of this. I want you to say my name," I growled.

June looked at me and lasciviously nibbled on her lower lip.

"John," she moaned as the candle wax covered her left bud.

"I love it when you say my name." Especially so full of lust. June desired me, just as much as I desired her. The way she looked at me so lustfully, even a bit more. Because unlike her, I could touch her body anytime. I could do whatever I wanted with June, while she wasn't allowed to move. With restraints, the fun would only be half as great, because then she would have no other choice. But without restraints, she had to make the choice herself not to want a choice.

"Is it difficult?" I asked. If June answered *yes* now, I would release her. I kept quiet about the fact that my erection was becoming painfully hard, because she should continue to see the dominant cowboy who was in control.

"Why? Do you need a break?" June panted and grinned at me.

Damn, she was really trying to drive me crazy.

Okay, baby. No problem. But I'm taking you with me!

"No, but when I'm done with you, you'll need a break. A damn long break."

I took off my shirt because the air was burning, crackling.

"Close your eyes." My command echoed through the silence of the night that had fallen over us. Only the remaining candles still provided us with light. I removed a spur from my shoe. Normally I rode without spurs, but today I had a feeling they might be useful. And they were, as I noted with pleasure. With my index finger, I turned the small silver wheel at the end of which were dozens of small spikes. Even the slightest touch with it was enough to turn a wild mustang into a gentle pony. What would it do to June then?

June waited patiently for me. Her eyes were closed, but her eyelids fluttered excitedly. With each second, her curiosity grew.

"Actually, I should have fucked you long ago. But since you don't need a break..." I growled, leaving a pregnant pause. "I'll take a little more time."

June tried not to show it, but she failed. I could see exactly how hungry she was, how much she wanted my cock.

I placed the silver spur on her forearm and gently rolled it up to her shoulders. It took all of June's strength not to move. Her flawless skin was sensitive, and I knew exactly which spots were even more sensitive.

I increased the pressure on my improvised Wartenberg wheel and circled her round breasts. June's chest rose and fell rapidly.

"Challenging?" I asked mockingly. I enjoyed this sight, no, damn it, I loved it! Keeping June so close between heaven and hell, pleasure and pain, dominance and submission was incredible.

June didn't answer, and she didn't need to. I could see every emotion on her face. No matter how hard she tried, I always saw through her facade and saw her real feelings behind it. Including her feelings for me, which had never changed.

The closer I got to her stiff buds, the sharper she inhaled. As hot as June was, she was just as stubborn, not moving an inch.

Good, stubborn girl.

I moved the small, pointed wheel over her stomach, down to her mound, and June gasped.

"John, please take me," she moaned. Her pleading was music to my ears.

What man didn't like to hear that he should relieve a woman?

"Can't you take it anymore?" I asked as the wheel wandered deeper.

"No! I can't take it anymore. I feel like I'll burn up if you don't take me right now."

Just before the silver wheel reached her most sensitive spot, I paused, then rolled back up to her navel.

I watched with a smile as June writhed in her lust. Now she didn't care if she moved or not. She gave in to her desire before she exploded.

"Did I give you permission to move?" I asked huskily. I licked her neck, which tasted sweet and salty.

"No. You didn't. Punish me for it. Punish me however you want, I don't care. But punish me later!"

"What a tempting offer," I answered with a smile. "I'll punish you however I want?"

"Yes! Do whatever you want with me, I'll do anything, really anything."

June had no idea how much power she was offering me - in her frenzy.

"I'll take you up on that," I murmured. Then I took off my jeans, knelt between her legs, and breathed a kiss on her most sensitive spot.

Damn, June was more than ready for me. I rubbed my hard erection against her soft skin. June thrust her hips toward me, looked at me, and fucked me with her eyes. The lust and the madness that lust led to burned in her eyes.

I grabbed her hips and thrust my cock deep into her in one go.

June screamed. With pleasure. With relief. With madness.

Her tightness massaged me and tempted me to thrust even harder into her, which June welcomed with loud moans.

June lay beneath me. Actually, I was more of a fan of doggy style or - cowboy that I was - the cowgirl position. But with June, I especially loved the missionary position. Because there, her petite, feminine body lay buried under my mountains of muscle. Safe, secure, and meant only for me.

With her mouth slightly open and a fuck-me look, June gazed at me. I returned her gaze and enjoyed how she massaged my cock with her movements while I remained still inside her.

My stubborn, good girl couldn't get enough of me, and I rewarded her lust with a series of hard, deep thrusts.

June wrapped her legs around my hips so I could penetrate even deeper. My cock wanted to penetrate her as deeply as possible. Given my size and her tightness, this wasn't easy, but it felt all the better when we did it.

"Oh, John," June moaned, close to orgasm. More words were on her lips, swallowed by her moans, but that was okay. I could read lips.

"I know, baby. I feel the same way," I murmured.

I thrust again and again while massaging her most sensitive spot with my right hand. The candlelight bathed June's silky skin in a golden-red glow. I followed the flickering light on her body with my tongue. Then I felt the trembling that passed from her body to mine, and we both came. Hard. Intense. Uncontrollable.

I lingered for a moment, enjoying our close body contact. June's breath came quickly, and with each breath escaped a soft moan.

"I love lying on you like this," I murmured.

"When I'm between your strong arms, I feel safe," June replied, and I smiled.

"And you know what else I love?" I asked rhetorically. Then I let myself fall to the side, panting, and grabbed June as if she were my prey. Now she nestled her round bottom against my cock while I could bury my nose in her fragrant hair.

June snuggled her back against my stomach, and I put my arm around her upper body. Her warm breath became calmer, yet still left goosebumps on my arms.

Incredible that after all this time, this anger, I could get so close to June again. I wanted more of it, and I wanted it forever. This thing between us wasn't a summer romance, it was meant for eternity, and somehow I had to convince June of that.

"I'll do it, under one condition," I murmured as I brushed a strand of hair from her face.

"Do what?" June asked sleepily.

"I'll compete with you in team roping."

"Really?" June looked at me with wide eyes. "And what's the condition?"

"We win the prize money. I'm certainly not making a fool of myself for second place," I said, winking at her.

Even though my pride saw it differently, I would take last place in every damn competition if only June would stay with me. Let the others see me as the nation's loser, June was the only grand prize I wanted.

Chapter 11 – June

T̲h̲e̲ P̲e̲a̲r̲s̲o̲n̲s̲'̲ s̲u̲m̲m̲e̲r̲ f̲e̲s̲t̲i̲v̲a̲l̲ was always well-attended, but it had never been as crowded as this year. All of Merryville, including all in-laws and extended family, was here.

John and I drove across the grounds in the pickup truck with a trailer to unload the horses. John drove at an agonizingly slow pace past dozens of groups of people, and I slid down in my seat as far as I could.

"What are you doing?" John asked with interest, without taking his eyes off the road.

"Hiding," I answered honestly.

"From whom?"

"These people here," I sighed.

"They don't bite. You know most of them," John joked and winked at me.

Yes, that's exactly the problem. I know everyone.

Of course, word had long since spread that I was back in Merryville, ever since I had eaten an apple crumble pie at Sue's Diner on the day of my arrival. And people had realized I wouldn't be disappearing again anytime soon when I started the holiday ranch with Red Rivers. That's exactly why I didn't want to have any uncomfortable conversations about how I could leave my successful business in New York unattended for weeks.

First, I led Champ out of the trailer, who immediately knew what was going on. I hadn't seen the fire in his eyes for a long time. And even though I wasn't keen on conversations, I could hardly wait for the competition.

Elli came waving towards us just as John was leading Phoenix out of the trailer.

"So, excited yet?" Elli asked, beaming.

"A little," I replied, patting Champ's neck. "But we're old hands in show business."

"And what about you, John? Excited?"

"Hm. No. I've already seen a large part of our competition. I'm certainly not afraid of them." John pulled me and Elli a step away from the horses, which were tied to one of the metal barriers. "As I said, I'm not worried about the competition," John began before being interrupted by Elli.

"Shh. Phoenix is ready. And he's great. Trust me, you'll fly out of the starting gates!"

I patted John on the shoulder. "If Elli says he's ready, then he's ready."

Elli thanked me with a broad grin. Then she fixed John with a serious look. "You can apologize to me after your victory."

"Keep dreaming, sis," John grumbled, then groomed Phoenix.

Elli looked at her watch. "Do you know where Sophia is?"

"She's getting our starting number," I answered. I didn't mention that I had pushed Sophia to do it. But I didn't want to see Rachel's face today before my comeback and our victory.

"Okey-dokey, then I'll go look for her. And if I happen to pass by that hot dog stand again, I might grab three or four for myself."

I giggled and waved goodbye to Elli. "See you later."

While John checked the horseshoes, I inspected the saddles for cracks. A good round lasted less than fifteen seconds. A lost horseshoe or a torn stirrup would cost valuable time.

The first names and starting numbers were being called out, while a band at the other end of the grounds provided feel-good music.

John wrapped his arms around me from behind, and I flinched.

"Is my roping champion nervous?" he asked. I flinched a second time.

"Yes," I answered with a husky voice. Not because of the competition, but because of the rumors we would set off with our ride.

"We shouldn't do this in public," I said and tried to break free from his embrace. In vain, John's arms were far too strong for me to have a chance.

He kissed my neck again. Slowly and sensually. His breath left goosebumps on my neck even in the sunny ninety degrees.

"You mean this?" he murmured. He kept covering my neck with kisses. My head screamed *no*, while my body shouted *yes*.

"Yes, exactly this," I answered.

His hands wandered to my hips, and he pressed himself harder against me.

What was he doing? He was turning me on. He was making me hungry. And this in the middle of the Pearson property, with thousands of people who could see us!

"John!" I sighed as he rubbed his erection against my behind. "People are already looking!"

"Let them look, I don't care."

"But then they'll talk," I whispered.

"Then let them talk. The opinion of people you barely know can't possibly matter to you."

"I'm afraid it does," I sighed.

John let go of me, but only to turn me around. Then he looked me straight in the eyes.

"I couldn't care less what others think. You shouldn't care either."

"I know, but it's difficult. Especially after New York. No one there defines you by what you are, how friendly and helpful. Everyone only defines you by what you've achieved."

"Sounds like the wrong place for you."

I smiled, because I knew John would say something like that.

"New York has its nice sides too," I tried to defend the city where I had found nothing but lost everything.

"Okay, name five."

I wasn't prepared for that.

"Coffee on every street corner," I answered quickly.

"One." He leaned forward towards me. "Actually, I should have you count."

"For what?" I asked, confused.

"For every time my hand slaps your bare bottom. You remember your get-out-of-jail-free card you gave me?"

My cheeks turned red within a second. Of course, John had remembered what I had offered him in my delirium. And I was a woman of my word. But not now.

"Secondly, stores are open. Always."

Now I had to think longer.

"High-speed internet."

John placed his index finger on my lips.

"All things nobody needs."

John was right, and we both knew it. I should have listed things like love, friendship, home, but those weren't in New York. As hard as it was for me to admit, everything was in Merryville, more specifically at *Red Rivers*.

"Hey, guys," Sophia called from a distance, saving me from the uncomfortable confrontation between my feelings and reality.

"Hey," I called back, turning away from John.

"Don't think you're getting away with that," John whispered in my ear. So seductively that I almost longed for his punishment. "Maybe I'll cash in my favor right now by spanking your perfect ass. In public. So you learn that other people's opinions are worthless."

My cheeks turned red again. Not because of his words, but because of his look that made it clear he would do exactly that.

Oh God, what have I unleashed here?

Sophia waved the bib numbers that we had to stick on our backs later.

"Jeez, it's pretty busy up front," Sophia said, panting, before handing us the bib numbers. "You've got the highest double number, that brings luck!"

Forty-four. We were the last ones, I knew that even before Sophia could say anything.

"Shall we check out the competition?" Sophia asked. She looked to the end of the grounds where the team roping was taking place.

"Sure," John replied. "I'm interested to see who we'll be beating today."

"Is it possible that you're even more confident today than usual?" Sophia asked, grinning, and I laughed.

"There's no higher degree of John's confidence."

One look from him was enough, and I knew he would spank me on the spot if I kept teasing him. Again, I asked myself: Was that a threat or a promise? With John, the lines blurred, sometimes evoking the most contradictory feelings in me.

John cleared his throat.

"We're a damn winning team. June's talent, my confidence, Champ's agility," John listed.

"You forgot Phoenix," I stated matter-of-factly.

"And Phoenix. A horse that's no longer afraid of cows for three days. Presumably. What could possibly go wrong?"

Sophia and I giggled while John grinned audaciously.

"You guys get the horses ready. I'll go ahead and grab a hot dog, okay?" Sophia asked.

"Can you and Elli think of anything other than food?" John asked, grinning, and Sophia feigned outrage. "We've already lost Elli to the hot dog stand, we can't lose you too."

I laughed so loudly that Champ and Phoenix pricked up their ears.

"It's in our Key genes. The constant hunger is just as innate to us as our stubbornness," Sophia replied, giggling. Then she disappeared, still giggling, towards the hot dog stand, and we finished saddling the horses.

I breathed in deeply the scent of Champ, oiled leather, and dust. It smelled like home, like competition, like victory. I could hardly wait to finally land in the starting box. But that would still take a while. Forty-three participants were before us, Rachel had made sure of that. Now I remembered the fourth reason why New York was also nice. No Rachel Pearson far and wide. Instead, I had seen John on every street corner. Every man with broad shoulders and dark brown hair wore John's face for a second.

"Are you ready?" I asked.

"Almost. Relax, we still have plenty of time."

"Yeah, because we're the last ones," I sighed.

"That's great."

"Great? How do you figure that?" I looked at him critically.

"Because we're the best. And the best always go last to make it exciting."

"Or so they become worn out, tired, and bored and mess it up," I replied bitterly.

John walked around the horses, grabbed me by the shoulders, and pushed me back until my back hit the horse trailer.

"I told you I'm only participating to win. And I always get what I want. You should know that best."

"Do I?" I asked softly.

John smiled at me while his eyes flashed dark. "We both know that."

He planted a soft kiss on my lips, and sparks flew between us. A second kiss followed. Then he took my lower lip between his teeth and licked it until my legs went weak.

"Not now," I whispered weakly.

"Yes, right now," John murmured and continued kissing me.

"Not here," I tried again.

"Yes, right here." With profound eyes and a thoughtful look, John pierced me to my very core.

"Does that mean you're cashing in your get-out-of-jail-free card from me?" John led me around the trailer, opened the small door on the side, and looked at me expectantly.

"No. We both know you want me just as much. Right now and right here."

Oh God, John was absolutely right. I wanted him. I was completely fallen for John and couldn't do anything about it. The more I fought against my feelings, the stronger they became.

I was hopelessly lost, hopelessly in love, and hopelessly fallen.

Right now and right here.

Chapter 12 – John

I PULLED JUNE THROUGH the side door into the empty horse trailer, pressed her against the wall, and kissed her passionately.

"John," June gasped softly.

Instead of answering, I gazed deeply into her eyes. No one could deny the passion between us, just as no one could deny my hard erection, which would never disappear on its own. I grabbed June and pressed her against the hay bales stacked in the front part of the trailer, smelling of home.

How could June leave all of this behind for a stuffy, noisy, overcrowded city?

The thought of her returning there soon almost tore my heart apart for a second time.

"I want you," I panted. My erection was clearly visible through the fabric of my jeans. I placed June's hand on the bulge, eliciting a smile from her.

"This is so naughty," she whispered and kissed me again.

"Damn right," I murmured between kisses. June sighed and pressed her body tightly against mine. No matter where we were, we were drawn to each other. And now this attraction had become so strong that we were undressing each other.

June unbuttoned my jeans and knelt in front of me.

I tilted my head back and gasped. As soon as her tongue tip touched my cock, I immediately thought of her last blowjob. Back then, in broad daylight, tied up. I hadn't given her a choice then. Now she had a choice, and June decided to catapult our blowjob thrill to the next level, no, into the next sphere.

I looked down at her as she licked my erection. Her emerald eyes were shining.

The large trailer door behind us, through which we had loaded the horses, was closed. No one could see us, but everyone could hear us.

Damn, it was exciting.

With June, I could live out my deepest and most hidden desires because deep down, we had the same fantasies. In June, they were just a little more hidden than in me.

But don't worry, baby. I'll bring your dirty cravings to light for you.

June's full, soft lips enveloped my tip, and she began to suck.

I sharply inhaled and braced myself against the hay bales.

"Damn, you're so good, baby."

She took my cock into her throat as deep as she could and held it there until she needed to breathe again.

Fuck.

June licked along my shaft with her tongue, never breaking eye contact.

"I wish I was tied up again," June whispered.

"So you like being helpless on your knees in front of me, at my mercy?" I murmured.

"I like being able to choose to be helpless."

Then June took my cock in her mouth again.

I had known from the start that my sweet little June was into hard, uninhibited sex. I could see it in her eyes. Girls who were into that kind of thing, girls like June, had that special glint in their eyes that other women would never have.

Carefully, I unbuttoned June's shirt to get a glimpse of her perfect breasts. Normally, I would have just torn the shirt off her body, but she still needed the blouse later. June belonged to me, her heart belonged to me, her breasts belonged to me. You don't share paradise - no one should even get a glimpse of it.

Damn, yes, I was in paradise.

I stood there, enjoying. Her seductive glances, her sensual sighs, her warm mouth, her skilled tongue, her tight throat.

"What other secret, forbidden, and depraved fantasies do you have?" I murmured.

"I'm not telling," June answered with a grin. "But you could find out."

Over the speakers that were placed everywhere, the starting numbers for team roping were being called. Even though I didn't want to, we had to hurry. Otherwise, I would have fucked June in the trailer all morning.

We simply couldn't keep our hands off each other. No matter how hard I tried, a single glance was enough to give me a raging hard-on.

"Come here," I commanded, pulling June up by her hands and undoing her jeans.

June bent forward and braced herself on the hay bale while I entered her from behind.

Tight. Hot. Ready.

Sometimes I felt like June was ready for me all day, so I could fuck her whenever it suited me.

I took June with hard thrusts. Her breathing was quick, and her body trembled with lust.

She tried to suppress her moans but didn't quite manage it.

"Quiet, baby. Or do you want someone to hear us?"

"I thought you didn't care about other people's opinions?" June countered.

I grinned. "Ten strikes."

"Let's make it twenty."

Damn, I loved that June had a mind of her own. And I loved how quickly she had understood how our game worked.

I thrust my cock even harder into her while reaching forward to her breasts, taking her nipples between my thumb and forefinger.

"You really should be quiet now," I warned June, then pinched her nipples hard.

June held her breath and glared at me with fiery, angry eyes, but she bravely bit her lips and remained silent.

Again and again, I released the pressure on her buds, only to increase it right after. Her body trembled more and more, and her breathing became increasingly irregular.

As tense and aroused as June was, she was also tight. Her walls massaged my erection, and it wouldn't be long before I couldn't help but give in to my orgasm.

"Come for me, baby," I murmured. I let go of her buds, grabbed her by the hips, and fucked her as hard as I could. The whole damn trailer shook, but I didn't stop until June complied with my wish and was flooded by an orgasm. She clenched so tightly around my erection that I couldn't help but spurt into her.

I rested my head briefly on her back to catch my breath.

Damn, that was...

"Incredible," June sighed softly, completing my thoughts.

"Yeah," I murmured. Then I pulled out of June and closed my pants. "We have to go."

June blew a brown strand of hair from her face as she buttoned up her blouse. Even through the thick fabric, her buds were clearly visible. The way I had treated them, June would feel them for quite a while - and I would see them for quite a while.

"I hope you've realized now that starting last has its advantages too, right?" I asked, grinning.

"If we had started first, you'd still be fucking me," June replied, smiling sweetly at me.

I raised an eyebrow and clicked my tongue disapprovingly.

What a little naughty girl.

Fortunately, I knew how to handle small, mischievous girls.

She expected me to say something, maybe threaten her with more spanks or tell her what other depraved things I had in mind for her, but I said nothing.

A gentleman enjoyed and kept quiet. Especially when he could drive the lady crazy by doing so.

I loved it when June looked at me the way she did in this moment. So intense and fiery. June had challenged me, and I accepted the challenge. But on my terms, by my rules, and to my advantage.

Baby, there are no losers with me. But I also don't allow you to win.

June snorted, then stepped out of the trailer's side door, grabbed Champ, and mounted up.

"Are you planning to take root or are you finally coming?" June asked teasingly, as if nothing had ever happened in the trailer where I was still standing.

"On my way."

I untied Phoenix, mounted up, and took one last look at the trailer.

We had managed to fuck in there unnoticed. Winning the tournament surely wouldn't be a problem after that.

"Next time, I'll make sure we start first, okay?" I broke my silence. June looked at me with wide eyes.

"Next time?"

"Why not? There are plenty of competitions we could enter. We make a good team and could take home any prize."

Although we had only trained for a few days, we were in perfect harmony. It would be a shame to give that up. Initially, I had only agreed because of the prize money, but I wanted to spend more time with June, no matter how.

June smiled at me painfully. "We'll see."

Damn, I had asked my question too soon. To participate in tournaments, June would have to be here, and for that, she'd have to put her life in New York on hold. Her look told me she wasn't ready for that yet. So I cleared my throat, adjusted my cowboy hat, and swallowed the lump in my throat.

I rode ahead, towards the competition, and June followed me.

"We still need to stop by the hot dog stand to pick up my sisters."

"I wish I could sin as much as your sisters," June sighed and caught up.

I raised an eyebrow questioningly. "We just sinned. How much more sinful do you want it to be?"

June's cheeks flushed. "That's not what I meant!"

"I know," I replied, winking at her. "I think your figure is perfect. And I find it pretty sexy when you take a hearty bite out of a burger."

We kept encountering riders in English style, warming up for the show jumping tournament taking place at the other end of the estate. At the same time as the team roping. I had no idea why, but here in

Texas, Western and English riders separated strictly, like the restaurant bill of a bad first date.

While we had juicy steaks and burgers, the elite over there ate appetizers that couldn't fill anyone up.

We had good music for celebrating and dancing, while the other side had oppressive violin fiddling.

How did the Pearsons come up with the idea to combine these tournaments every year?

Anyway, I was glad to be on the fun side of the summer festival. With greasy burgers, good music, and June. We rode past square dancers, and at the beer tables, the bronc riders were already drunk, even though the rodeo wasn't until the afternoon. Kids were also practicing lasso swinging on hay bales with plastic horns stuck to them.

"If I missed anything, it was this," June said, taking a deep breath as if she wanted to inhale the atmosphere.

"What about me?" I asked.

"You're part of it," June answered seriously. "You. Champ. The sun. The crackle in the air just before the start. Everything."

I should have told her she could stay, but I couldn't. June wasn't ready for the truth yet. Maybe she'd never be ready for it, but I could still give her a little more time.

"It's nice that you're here," I said instead. "By the way, I still have my get-out-of-jail-free card. So you should behave and be a good girl."

June laughed out loud. "You must be dreaming."

"I'm currently dreaming about fucking your brains out behind the bleachers."

"John!" June exclaimed, scandalized.

"And that's exactly how you moan my name. Over and over again, until I allow you to come."

"You can't do that," June whispered.

"Yes, I can. I could also use my get-out-of-jail-free card to tie you up in all sorts of ways in the hayloft. Ropes look so good on you," I murmured.

June's cheeks grew increasingly red.

"I can do whatever I want with you," I growled like a hungry wolf. The fire I had ignited in her emerald eyes blazed uncontrollably.

Before June could answer, we spotted the hot dog stand where my sisters had staged a true hot dog massacre.

Kate, a waitress from Sue's Diner who was running the hot dog stand, waved at me with a laugh.

"John, get these two off my back, or there won't be any hot dogs left until the afternoon!"

"Hey," Elli protested with a giggle. "We're paying for them. That's no way to treat your best customers."

Sophia, her mouth still full, nodded eagerly.

"We need you guys as support," June said with a smile.

"That's right, we should accompany the winning team to the start," Sophia said, smiling as she finished her last hot dog.

With Elli and Sophia walking between us, we made our way to the tournament area for team roping. The crowd in the stands was cheering so loudly that we didn't need any signs to find our competition.

The stands surrounded a large, fenced-in area where pairs of riders were catching cattle. Over the loudspeaker, the team with starting number thirty-nine was just being called.

"What's the best time so far?" June asked, critically eyeing the competition.

"Seven seconds and change," Sophia answered.

Elli grinned at us. "You'll beat that easily."

"Seven seconds is pretty good," June replied seriously.

She was right. Seven seconds was a damn good time.

"And you're better," Elli insisted with crossed arms. I shared her opinion.

"As our coach, you have to say that," I replied with a grin.

"As your coach, I'm saying that your best time was six seconds and you're going to win."

While June analyzed the competition with Sophia, I kept a close eye on Phoenix. He wasn't used to the competition hubbub. Even though he wasn't afraid of cattle at home anymore, that didn't mean he wouldn't be afraid of them anywhere else.

"Phoenix is ready," Elli said, stroking Phoenix's head.

I patted his neck. Even though I sometimes made fun of the white horse, we had trained hard. There had been a few setbacks, but we needed the prize money.

"Yeah, damn right."

"You too."

Elli looked in June's direction.

"What are you talking about?" I asked.

"And June especially is."

"I have no idea what you're talking about. Are you feeling okay? Do you have a fever? Or is this one of your secret girl codes for 'I need more hot dogs'?" I joked.

Elli looked at me desperately. "You're an idiot if you don't know what I'm talking about."

"The last team, with the starting number forty-four, please proceed to the starting position."

"Oh, that's us!" June called out excitedly. She urged Champion past me and grinned. "Champ and I are on a lucky streak. Seventeen wins in a row. Don't you dare let us down."

I looked at her seriously, thinking of only one thing.

Get out of jail free.

But even that couldn't diminish her grin.

A gate was opened on the western side of the fence, through which we could ride onto the field.

We stood at the end of the field, me on the left side, June on the right. And between us stood a steer in a box, just waiting to dash away from us.

The crowd waited eagerly for the referee's final announcement before it all began.

"I think I know now what I'll use my free pass for," I muttered.

"John. Not. Here."

"Trust me, baby. That's exactly what you'd answer too."

"Focus, John," June scolded me, laughing.

"Okay, okay," I gave in. "But only until after the tournament. Then I want to use my... *freedom* with you."

Now June laughed even louder. Then the speakers crackled and conversations everywhere fell silent.

"In the last team competing today, we have John Key riding Phoenix and - who doesn't know our cutting legend - June Farley on Champion of Tournament. The current best time to beat is seven point three four seconds."

The crowd cheered for us. I loved it. Damn, there was no better feeling than showing the whole damn world that June and I belonged together.

"It feels good to hear our full names from the loudspeakers," June gushed, looking at me over the steer. "Ready?"

"Ready," I answered. And suddenly I understood what Elli had meant earlier.

I'm damn ready.

We got set to start. I took a deep breath. The dusty air scratched my lungs.

In the next seven seconds, we could decide whether June would stay longer to finish the vacation rentals, or if she'd return to New York right away.

I patted Phoenix's soft coat one last time.

If a cattle-phobic horse could suddenly become a roping horse, even though no one - except Elli - had believed in it, then there was hope for me too.

That's what Elli had meant earlier.

"Don't let me down, Phoenix," I whispered to the white horse.

I took his short snort as a *never, buddy*.

Our victory was proof of everything. Suddenly, this victory meant not just a win, it meant everything.

It was time. The box opened and the steer shot out like a torpedo. June and I immediately gave chase. I swung my lasso, trusting Phoenix to do his job - keep chasing the steer. He didn't disappoint me, and a second later my lasso had wrapped around the bull's horns.

"Yes!" I shouted, as I brought Phoenix to a stop, forcing the bull to turn around too. Now it was June's turn. Her job was significantly harder than mine, as she had to catch the running bull's hind legs with the lasso. And do it in less than seven seconds.

June swung the lasso with concentration, and when she threw it, the world moved in slow motion. My entire future was being decided by a single second and a ridiculous lasso. Absurd! And yet so real that it almost scared me.

The lasso flew slower and slower, while my heart hammered faster and faster. It wouldn't be long before my heart exploded. Against better judgment, I closed my eyes, held my breath, and waited for the referee's announcement.

"What a beautiful ride," he commented over the loudspeaker. The guy was a torturer, making us wait so long for the time. He praised my swing, June's comeback, and even talked about Phoenix's phobia.

The time, damn it! I'm on the verge of a heart attack!

"Let's move on to the time. I can hereby announce that June Farley and John Key have secured victory with six point seven three seconds."

My eyes widened. "We won!"

"Shit, yes! We won!" June swore with joy.

"What kind of language is that for a city girl?" I asked, grinning.

"I'm not a city girl, I'm a cowgirl," she replied seriously, touching the brim of her hat. "Remind me to never wear anything but boots again."

June, naked, wearing only cowboy boots? Yeah, I liked that.

I grinned. "My pleasure."

Although the crowd around us was cheering and applauding loudly, I only had eyes for June.

We were a perfect team. Everyone saw that. And now we had proof of it.

Had June and I been so blind that everyone saw how deep our connection was, except for us?

As befitting true winners, we galloped a lap around the entire arena to wave at the crowd. When we returned to the center, I swung euphorically out of the saddle so we could immediately claim our trophy, and June did the same.

"You know what, June?" I asked.

"What?"

"I want to use my *Get Out of Jail Free Card* now."

She snorted, but I took her hand and looked at her seriously.

"I mean it. I want to use it. Now."

"And what do you want?"

"A kiss. Here and now," I murmured.

"What?!"

"You're right. I do care what people think. I want everyone here to know that we love each other. June Farley, we're meant for each other, every damn idiot can see it, only we're still fighting against it."

June looked deep into my eyes. I could see her thoughts racing and her heart pounding wildly. She bit her lower lip thoughtfully. I understood how difficult this was for June because she was deciding the future for both of us. But considering it was about her and me, it should be easy for her.

We. Belong. Together. Period.

"Let me kiss you," I murmured once more.

Then she threw her arms around my neck and gave me a passionate kiss. Our tongues touched, sparks flew, and ignited a fire that no one would ever be able to extinguish.

Chapter 13 – June

"I still can't believe we won," I cheered while spoiling Champ with some extra grooming in his stall. Elli was tending to Phoenix in the neighboring stall, and Sophia was keeping us company.

"And I still can't believe you two finally kissed!" Elli added with a grin.

Yes, the kiss. When I thought about it, thousands of butterflies fluttered in my stomach. John and I had become the number one topic of conversation in Merryville. And not because of our victory in team roping.

"The best part was Rachel's face!" Sophia burst out laughing. "I swear to you, she turned poison green right up to her roots."

"That's not important. What's more important is that we can finally get the vacation rentals ready for occupancy," I replied seriously. Our eyes met, and we broke into laughter simultaneously.

Of course, the money was important to us, but the mental punch to Rachel's fake smile was my second biggest victory.

Rachel had been throwing me death glares one after another during the award ceremony. I should really be above all that had happened, but getting back at Rachel doubly through victory and a kiss felt good.

After the award ceremony, we walked hand in hand through the summer festival, and I felt proud to show the world that John belonged to me and I to him.

"Where's John anyway?" I asked. "He should have been here by now."

"Good question," Elli said dryly.

"I'll go look for him," I said, tossing the curry comb into the grooming box.

"No!" Sophia shouted so loudly that I flinched.

"No?" I asked, confused.

"No. I mean, I think you should give Champ a few more cuddles. After all, he's seamlessly continued your recent successes."

"True," I replied, smiling. I scratched Champ behind his ears, in the spot every horse loved.

"Back to Rachel's poison green face," Elli said, putting on her I'm-in-the-mood-for-gossip face. "It was really, really green!"

"And how!" Sophia added.

As our laughter slowly subsided, Sophia cleared her throat.

"Seriously though, your vacation houses are saving *Red Rivers*."

"Our vacation houses," I corrected Sophia with a smile. "This is our joint project. I got a distraction, and you'll soon be out of the red. Classic win-win situation."

Automatically, I felt guilty because I still hadn't told anyone about the real reasons for my escape from New York. But now wasn't a good time for that. We were all in a celebratory mood, and I didn't want to spoil it for anyone.

"And you're also getting a great, strong cowboy," Sophia joked.

"The greatest and strongest cowboy," Elli corrected her sister. Then they both burst out laughing.

"Did we just say something nice about John?"

Sophia put her finger to her lips. "Only under the seal of secrecy."

Elli looked at me through the bars of the stalls and raised her index finger threateningly.

"In case you tell John, we'll both deny everything."

I giggled. "I envy you for your family."

"Our family," Sophia said with a smile. "You've been a part of it for a long time now."

I was so touched that tears came to my eyes. It had always felt like I was at home here and part of the family, but knowing that the others felt the same way moved me immensely. This wasn't just my home and my family, but also my heart. I had never taken it with me to New York.

I cleared my throat. My vocal cords were still trembling so much that I couldn't say anything. But I didn't have to.

"Enough cuddles for today, Champ."

I patted the soft fur of his neck one last time, then left the stall.

Again, Sophia and Elli exchanged strange looks.

"I can't shake the feeling that you two are hiding something from me," I sighed.

"Us? Secrets? Nooo," Elli said, nodding vigorously.

"You're the worst liar I've ever seen," I replied, grinning.

"True. Don't listen to her. Listen to me. We're definitely not trying to buy time here," Sophia chimed in.

I laughed. "Okay Elli, I take it all back. You're only the second-worst liar in the world."

"Hey!" Sophia protested.

"It's okay," I said, raising my arms in a placating gesture. "I won't go looking for John. You've convinced me to just stay here and wait for nothing to happen."

I winked at the two of them, who visibly exhaled in relief.

"Then let's talk about something else," I said, looking around thoughtfully. My gaze settled on Prime Tribute's stall, a beautiful black stallion that had been here for a few days.

"How are things going with Rachel's other horses?" I asked Elli.

"Pretty good. It would be better if Rachel wasn't constantly keeping me from work."

"Wait and see. Maybe she's had enough of June and John's movie-worthy kiss," Sophia said with a smile.

"Hm," I mumbled softly. "Rachel can be really persistent when she doesn't get what she wants."

"Well, John wants you, not her. She can't have John, end of story," Elli sighed.

Sophia bit her lip thoughtfully. "Maybe it's not even about John for Rachel. At least not primarily."

I furrowed my brow pensively. "What do you mean by that?"

"Do you remember high school?"

"How could I forget."

"Then think about all the friends Rachel had."

When I realized what Sophia was getting at, I held my breath.

"She always wanted the guys who were already taken."

"Bingo."

I narrowed my eyes. "Wait. Does that mean she doesn't even want John, she just wants to steal him from me - again?"

"Yep," said Elli. "Since you disappeared from here, Rachel hasn't stopped by even once."

I admit, I hadn't dared to ask if John and Rachel had ever been a couple. It would have broken my heart.

"This time I'm not giving up so easily," I said, determined to fight.

"I hope so, for your sake," Sophia answered, grinning.

Elli nodded. "*Red Rivers* could use more girl power."

I grinned. The male-to-female ratio at *Red Rivers* was really high. Apart from Sophia, Elli, there were only their mom and grandma. Otherwise, just dozens of men living scattered across the houses.

"Where's John?" I tried a second time.

"We don't know," Elli answered innocently.

She and John had definitely cooked up something. But what?

"Okay, okay. I give up. Just tell me how things are going with Prime Tribute."

I leaned against the stall door and glanced at the black horse. He looked beautiful and so noble that he was surely worth more than all of *Red Rivers*.

"He's amazing. I've never seen a dressage horse with such gaits. He floats across the arena." Elli leaned forward towards Sophia and me and whispered: "And I think he can read minds. He starts doing things before I've even finished thinking them."

"Why are you whispering?" I asked, laughing.

"So he can't hear me."

"That makes absolutely no sense," Sophia burst out laughing.

"Yes, it does," Elli defended herself.

While Elli and Sophia were discussing whether a sentence could be spoken without thinking about it, I stroked Prime Tribute's nostrils.

"Why is he here?" I asked.

"Because Rachel's afraid he'll read her thoughts and find out she doesn't have any," Elli answered, grinning.

"Sis, you're confusing her thoughts with her feelings."

"Rachel jokes never get old," I giggled.

"True," Sophia replied.

"So, Elli. What's the deal with Prime Tribute?"

"He's lonely. But he doesn't get along with other horses."

"Phew, tough problem," I sighed.

"Oh yeah," Elli snorted. "We're making zero progress. If this keeps up, Rachel will soon move in here. For good." Almost as if Prime Tribute had been listening, he tossed his head up and snorted heavily.

"I don't blame you," Elli said quickly. Then she held her hands in front of her lips. "See, he can read minds!"

I nodded. "I admit, that was creepy."

"As long as he keeps our thoughts to himself, I wouldn't worry," Sophia joked.

We continued chatting, laughing at jokes, and tending to the horses together until dusk.

"I know you won't tell me what John's up to. But you don't have to pretend you're distracting me. I can just act totally surprised when John finally shows up."

"We're not distracting you," Elli answered, grinning.

Fine, so they wanted to keep playing the game. Whatever. I didn't have anything else to do anyway.

"Alright then. I'll sweep the stable aisle. And remind me never to hire you two as secret distractions," I said, grinning, then grabbed the broom.

"We don't know what you're talking about, June," Sophia replied, smiling.

"Of course not." I winked at her.

"Is Nougat outside with the others?" Elli asked, leaning against the empty stall.

"No, I didn't let her out," Sophia answered. They both looked at me and I shook my head.

"I didn't let Nougat out of the stall either."

Elli snorted loudly. "Good Lord, this goat is driving me crazy."

"You didn't let her out to distract me longer, did you?" I asked, confused. At this point, I wouldn't put anything past those two.

"No, of course not!" Sophia said seriously.

Okay. Judging by her look, Nougat wasn't a distraction tactic, but an escapee - again.

It took us nearly twenty minutes to find her bleating indignantly in the hayloft, which was supposedly only accessible by ladder.

"This goat can walk up walls, I swear," Elli said, shaking her head.

"You still haven't figured out who she belongs to?" I asked.

"No. Our vet has no idea, and nobody responded to the flyers in town. I guess she'll be keeping us on our toes for a while longer," Sophia answered, stroking the goat's head.

After we'd brought Nougat back to her stall, and there was still no sign of John, Sophia and Elli took drastic measures by deciding we should oil all the saddles and bridles.

My fingers were aching when John finally showed up.

"John, there you are at last!"

Overjoyed, I fell into his arms. "You should greet me like this more often," John murmured and planted a kiss on my cheek.

"I will if you never make me wait this long again."

"What are you doing?" John asked, interested.

"We're oiling the leather," Elli and Sophia said in unison.

John growled loudly. "You couldn't come up with a better distraction?"

Elli and Sophia exchanged a quick glance, then pierced John with reproachful looks.

Sophia put her hands on her hips, while Elli snorted.

"If you hadn't taken so long for - whatever - we wouldn't have had to resort to such drastic measures," Sophia defended herself and her sister.

I bit my lip to keep from laughing out loud.

"Calm down, guys. We should finally celebrate our victory now," I tried to quash the discussion.

John put his arm around my shoulders. "We should. But first, I have to show you something."

I looked at Sophia and Elli, who both nodded conspicuously inconspicuously.

"Okay." I gave John my hand and let him lead me outside.

"You need to change your clothes," John said, and I looked down at myself. What was wrong with my jeans and blouse? My outfit was fancy enough to participate in a tournament and casual enough to eat a burger at Sue's.

"And what should I wear?" I asked.

"The dress you wore on the day you arrived," John murmured.

I looked at him with a frown. "Why?"

John gave me a calm smile. "Because I like it."

I didn't know what to make of this smile, nor what John had planned. I tried not to show my excitement.

"Give me ten minutes."

"Five." John looked at me seriously. That look left no room for discussion.

"Five," I repeated and ran into the house to change.

Five minutes! John really had no idea how long it took women to get ready to go out. There wasn't enough time for makeup or brushing my hair. In the chaos of my suitcase, I didn't even have enough time to find matching underwear. And I still needed to find my shoes!

I had to make a choice. Either matching underwear or matching shoes.

Damn compromises!

When I was ready, I left the house with black heels and red cheeks.

Elli and Sophia, who had been waiting with John on the porch, grinned at me with the same mischievous expression.

"You look enchanting," John said and took my hand. His skin felt rough and warm against mine.

I thanked him with a shy smile and let him lead me to his pickup.

"See you later," Sophia said goodbye and headed towards the main house.

John waved back at them. "Don't wait up for us. It might be late. Or tomorrow."

"Okey-dokey," Elli called out, following Sophia.

"Until tomorrow? What are you planning?" I asked curiously.

Neither Sophia nor Elli had revealed what John had planned. But judging by how they behaved, it was something big. The butterflies in my stomach fluttered excitedly.

His eyes darkened and his gaze became serious.

"You'll find out soon enough," John murmured and handed me a blindfold made of black silk. "But I'll tell you one thing: Your wish for twenty strikes will soon be fulfilled."

Chapter 14 – John

WE STOOD IN FRONT of my pickup and June looked at me with wide eyes. Her pupils dilated as I mentioned the twenty strokes. Good. I loved seeing her sweet ass get spanked. Even better that June enjoyed it just as much.

I had ordered her to wear the black dress that I had wanted to rip off her body from the first moment I saw her. She looked enchanting in it.

June let the silk blindfold slide through her fingers and bit her lower lip thoughtfully.

"Where are you taking me?" June asked.

A soft murmur escaped my throat and I smiled. Just thinking about where I was taking June made my cock twitch.

"I would never want to spoil the surprise. Do you trust me enough to follow me blindly?" I whispered, looking at the blindfold.

"I would follow you anywhere," June replied with a smile. I loved her for the look she gave me in that moment. A look that said she trusted me.

Damn, I would never let June go again, even if I had to follow her to the ends of the earth. We were made for each other.

June put on the blindfold and I helped her tie it. Carefully, I helped June into my pickup and drove off.

"I'm really curious," June sighed.

"You're allowed to be. I have a lot planned for you," I murmured.

My little girl had no idea what was about to happen. She couldn't, because my sisters had no clue. At least not about the official part of my plan. Of course, I had to reveal a few small details to them, but June and I would only get to that much later.

I placed my free hand on her bare thigh and stroked her delicate skin. The ride wouldn't be long, but I couldn't hold back any longer. I needed a little taste of what was waiting for me. Slowly, without taking my eyes off the road, I slid June's dress up until my hand slipped between her legs. Instinctively, June spread her legs and arched her back. She sighed softly and sensually, but the higher my hands traveled, the louder she became.

When I felt that June wasn't wearing any underwear under her dress, I growled with pleasure.

"You're not wearing any panties? What a nice surprise," I said.

"I didn't have time," June admitted.

"I like it when you don't have time," I growled. "You should go out without panties more often."

Or always, so I could get a look at her perfect ass whenever I wanted.

My fingers traveled down her Venus mound to her clit. I rubbed her sensitive pearl, making June moan even louder.

"Oh God!"

"We're almost there," I said, not stopping. I loved driving June crazy. A moan on the edge of madness was the second best thing for me. When we finally arrived at my destination, I would make June moan the most beautiful moan.

"Hopefully, I can hardly stand it," June whispered. Her legs trembled with desire. Damn, the situation had gotten June so aroused that she was almost coming.

"Not! Coming!" I commanded in a rough voice. But my fingers stayed where they were.

June took a deep breath and tried to relax.

"Good girl."

I steered the car onto the road leading to the holiday ranch I had slightly remodeled for my purposes. June would see that later. First, we had to visit the first, completed hut. Because I had also made a few small but significant changes there.

The sun had completely disappeared on the horizon by the time we arrived. But the string lights hanging on the porches and the campfire I had lit earlier provided enough light to see.

"We're here," I whispered. Then I got out, walked around the car, and helped June out. I enjoyed the view that presented itself to me, thanks to her dress having slipped up. June clung tightly to my shoulders because she couldn't get a good footing on the gravel in her heels.

"I love these shoes, baby. But you should only wear them in bed," I remarked.

Good thing we're on our way to a bed.

"I can walk in them," June protested.

"Sure," I replied sarcastically. Then I let go of June's hand, grabbed her by the waist, and threw her over my shoulder.

"John! Put me down right now!" June protested and flailed wildly. I could easily balance her light weight.

"Put me down!" she commanded for the second time, as I continued unperturbed toward the vacation cabin.

"Haven't you figured out yet that I'm the one giving the orders?" I asked.

"No!" Her resistance grew stronger. Now she wasn't just flailing but also pounding her fists against my back.

"Don't push it, my beauty," I threatened her with a serious, calm voice. June wasn't impressed.

I opened the door and carried June inside.

Damn, I loved it here. It was the first finished house, and June had outdone herself with the decor. Now, with my upgrades, it was perfect.

She stopped resisting only when I set her down on the wooden floor inside the cabin and took a step back.

Thanks to the blindfold, June couldn't see anything, so she stayed put while I circled around her like a wolf on the hunt.

"Take off your dress," I commanded.

"What?" June asked shyly. The rebel was gone, at least temporarily, and my devoted, innocent June remained, who still had a lot to learn.

"I want to see you!" I ordered. Of course, I could have just taken off her dress. June wouldn't have resisted. But I wanted her to undress herself, just like her devoted nature.

Slowly, June slipped her dress off her shoulders. It slid down her body and onto the floor.

"I love your perfect body," I whispered in her ear as I continued to circle around her. I wanted to explore every single inch. June was simply perfect. And the best part was: every single inch belonged to me, foremost her heart.

"On your knees!"

June obeyed my command and knelt devotedly before me. She had instinctively lowered her head.

With my finger, I traced her full lips, which she slightly parted, allowing my finger to glide over her tongue. When she closed her mouth around my finger and sucked on it, I let out a soft moan. She was a natural talent. Her sensual lips and skillful tongue made me anticipate what was to come. Pure, honey-sweet sins that would grant us access to all imaginable places. But before that, we had to surrender to madness. Not just June had to control herself, but also me. It was getting tight in my pants. I would have loved to fuck June right there, but not without trying out part of my apartment upgrades.

So much time had to be.

As June sucked on my finger, I glanced at the bed. Various whips, paddles, and sticks that I had procured in the city lay there. Also, ropes of different lengths. Candles burned on the nightstands, not only providing romantic lighting but also for sensual screams.

On the bed itself, I had attached several hooks to the posts, where I could fasten ropes or leather cuffs. In front of the bed, I had installed a hook in the ceiling to tie June up standing or to attach a love swing that was waiting under the bed for its use.

I pulled my finger out of her mouth and lifted her chin, turning her face left and right. June had the most beautiful face in the world.

"I will never let you go again," I made clear.

"And I will never run away again," June replied.

"No, you won't. I'll make sure of that."

That was a promise. I decided to show June every conceivable place. Every damn place in the world, all the seas, and if I had my way, the entire universe, just to prove that her place was by my side.

"Do you know where we are?" I asked.

"We're at the vacation ranch," June answered.

"Almost right. We're standing at the edge. And you're just one decision away from me leading you over it. But I swear to you, you won't fall, you'll fly. You just have to trust me."

"I trust you," June replied resolutely.

"Good."

I took one of the whips from the bed. It was short and not very flexible. At the end was a wide, curved piece of leather that made a wonderful sound when it hit bare skin.

I let the whip whistle through the air several times, and June flinched with each stroke. Smiling, I let the leather tip of the whip glide over June's cheek as if it were a feather.

"You've never experienced a whip before, have you?"

"No," June whispered.

I smiled contentedly. So, I was the first man to show June the pleasure of pain. It would be a revelation for her, I was sure of that.

"Are you afraid?" I continued to ask.

"No." There was something else on her tongue, but June bit her lip before she could say it.

"What else did you want to say?" I asked.

"It's ... " June began but then stopped. June was usually a damn quick-witted, confident girl. Seeing her so shy and reserved was a real surprise to me. But I had immediately known that her submissive side suited her just as well as her confidence.

"It's simple," I added to her sentence. "You kneel naked before me. Your body belongs to me. Show me that you really belong to me by sharing your secrets with me!"

June took a deep breath. "I've sometimes imagined being disciplined."

"Good girl." I whispered a kiss on her lips.

"You're not surprised?" June asked, irritated, and I smiled.

"No. Anyone who lets themselves be lassoed to be fucked by a cowboy, right out in the open field, obviously has a submissive side. You're lucky because, coincidentally, I have a pretty dominant side that I want to express."

I stroked June's arm with the whip to show her what to expect.

"You said twenty strokes, right?"

June nodded. "Yes."

"Ah, why be so stingy. Let's make it thirty," I said grinning.

Then I started the first stroke on her arm.

To June's surprise, my first strokes hardly hurt.

Wait, baby. This is the warm-up.

After June got used to the whip, my strokes became firmer. I didn't limit myself to her arms. Her thighs and flanks also gradually received light stripes.

"Stretch out your arms," I commanded and grasped June's wrists so I could guide them where I wanted them. Stretched out in front of her body, with her palms up, so I could hit both arms at once.

The whip hit the same spot over and over. With each stroke, June sucked in the air more sharply. My strokes were mean, I knew that, but June endured bravely until I took another break.

"Do you like it?" I asked, as only ten more strokes were due.

"Oh yes," she sighed.

I went down on my knees and stroked over June's bare torso. Her breasts swayed with each breath, and her nipples were stiff with arousal.

I spread her thighs apart and my hand slid between her legs.

Damn, she was more than ready. But she had to wait a little longer. The longer I could delay her pleasure, the greater my own desire became.

The waiting was cruel, but it led to the best orgasms in the world.

Fuck, I can't wait any longer.

I grabbed June, pulled her up, and pushed her towards the bed. She stood in front of it, and I bent her forward to support her upper body on the mattress.

Her high heels created a seductive arch, making her body look elegant and graceful.

I grabbed her ass from behind and massaged it. It was firm and taut, and soon it would glow fiery red.

The first strike took June by surprise, and she let out a loud moan. Startled by her volume, June bit her lip, and I clicked my tongue.

"You can scream as loud as you want. No one will hear you."

I struck again, but June stifled her scream once more.

"Scream for me," I commanded. Then the whip struck her skin with a resounding crack.

This time, June gave in and screamed, moaned, gasped.

Music in my ears.

"Say you belong to me!" I ordered in a hoarse voice.

"I belong to you," June whispered, and I smiled contentedly.

After the last strokes, beautiful red stripes formed on her ass.

"John?" June asked thoughtfully.

"Yes?"

"Show me that I belong to you!"

I leaned forward and nibbled on her ear.

"You belong to me," I whispered.

And my damn heart belongs to you.

I wanted to tell her that since our first encounter. But I still couldn't bring it to my lips. All I could do was show her my love.

My hand stroked her neck, and as I reached her shoulder blades, I pressed her down.

June stayed still. Not because she was a good girl, but because my weight kept her where I wanted her. Then I took the ropes lying next to June on the bed and tied them to her wrists. I increased the pressure on June's shoulders.

"Do you like it when I take what I want?" I asked.

"Yes!"

"Even when I want you?" I asked in a hoarse voice.

"Especially then," June replied with a smile. Even though June was submissive at the moment, she was also a fighter. Letting herself be bound by me required not only trust but also courage.

June was sometimes submissive, but also passionate and wild, and this mix gave our relationship the fire we both loved.

I grabbed June, threw her onto the bed, and tied the ropes so that June's hands were bound above her head to the bed frame. I also removed her blindfold. I wanted to see her eyes while I fucked her.

June blinked a few times until she got used to the candlelight. Her pupils were so large that the black had swallowed her green irises.

When I unzipped my pants and my erection sprang out, June licked her lips.

Normally, I would never say no to a good blowjob, but I was so horny that I couldn't wait any longer. I spread her legs, rubbed my hard cock against her wet entrance, and then thrust into her to the hilt.

Fuck. She was so tight...

Gasping, June wrapped her legs around my hips. She wanted it harder, deeper, and I was ready to fulfill that desire.

Our eyes met. I savored her greedy, wild gaze and the sensual moans I elicited with each thrust.

June clawed at her restraints, her entire body trembling with arousal.

"Oh God!" she gasped.

For June, it must have felt like a revelation, how all her feelings were intensified by the blows before. I had a whole series of revelations lined up for June.

Damn, I had stocked up with a year's supply of things. Nipple clamps, love balls, vibrators. Toys and whips that I would slowly introduce to June.

"Come for me, baby," I gasped.

June's orgasms triggered small orgasms in me too.

She fulfilled my wish, threw her head back, and let me fuck her as hard as she had ever been fucked before. June had tasted ecstasy, and now she couldn't get enough. That suited me well, because I was just as addicted as she was.

Addicted to my dominance.

Addicted to her submission.

Addicted to June.

Breathlessly, June came to herself again. I kept fucking her. And kept fucking her. And kept fucking her... until she came a second time. I was addicted to her orgasms. The moments when she gasped for air while her eyelids fluttered and her walls tightened so tightly around me that it took my breath away, burned into my memory.

I bent down to her, and our lips met. I licked over her seductive lips and pushed into her mouth. Our tongues played with each other. June tasted honey-sweet.

As I drove June to her third orgasm, I came too. Gasping, I pumped my gold into her.

Damn!

I let myself fall next to her on the bed to catch my breath. For a moment, there was only my orgasm and the beating of our hearts—they beat in the same rhythm.

"Do you want to let me go?" June asked after we had calmed down a bit.

"Do I want to?" I asked back. I looked her up and down and shook my head. "No, I don't." I liked it when June lay bound next to me. The restraints forced her body into enticing positions.

I would never admit it out loud, but as long as June was bound, I could be sure she wouldn't run away from me again.

"Yes, you do," June replied with a smile.

"Let me enjoy your sight for a while," I demanded. Then I stroked over the tender skin of her body.

"Okay." June looked around. We lay amidst whips and floggers, restraints, vibrators, clamps, and clothespins. Curiously, she eyed the nipple clamps connected by a chain. "What's that?"

"That's for your nipples. They create intense feelings. But we'll get to that later."

"Why later?"

"They're not for beginners like you," I replied with a smile.

June pouted. "I'm not a beginner."

Even though June was tough, I wanted to slowly introduce her to different kinds of pain. Nipple clamps were a whole different league than candle wax or a spring flogger.

June clearly couldn't get enough. Grinning, I lifted a ball gag.

"If you keep contradicting me, I'll use the gag. It's excellent for loud beginners."

June giggled. "No, I'll be good now."

"That's what I wanted to hear," I replied with a smile. I reluctantly untied her restraints and stood up. "Come on, I want to show you something."

Chapter 15 – June

John positioned himself behind me, covered my eyes from behind, and led me out of the cabin.

"Surprise," he said and revealed the view of the vacation homes.

"Oh, wow," I marveled. With a leap, I jumped off the porch and stood in the middle of the area where a campfire was crackling.

John had attached string lights to all the houses and nearby trees, bathing everything in romantic light. It looked like something out of a fairy tale.

"The houses aren't finished yet, but I think it's pretty good," John said.

"It's perfect," I corrected him, and he winked at me.

Incredible. One moment he was dominant and spanking me, and the next he was a hopeless romantic who knew exactly how to win my heart.

I turned around in a circle a few times to inspect the vacation homes more closely. It was truly perfect. It was real. It was home.

"My grandparents would have loved it," I said thoughtfully. Even though they couldn't see it, I knew they would have been proud of me.

"They would have," John replied. He took my hand and led me to the campfire, around which a few thick logs were placed.

"I'm really glad we have enough money to finish building the other apartments," I sighed. It would have broken my heart if our project had failed so close to completion.

"And I'm glad you stayed. We never would have managed this without you."

"Oh, come on," I waved it off. "You did most of the work. I just had a few visions and a bit more money."

John grabbed me by the shoulders and looked at me seriously.

"You had a dream and held onto it. And you helped us even though you didn't have to. You stayed even though you didn't have to."

My heart pounded wildly in my chest. Now would have been a good time to finally come clean with him, but I didn't dare. So I smiled at him and said, "Okay. I give up. Now let's finally celebrate our victory." I tried to get rid of my overwhelming thoughts through laughter.

"Damn right. Who would have thought Phoenix would really overcome his fear of cows?"

"Elli," I said dryly. Then we both laughed.

"Touché. Admittedly, I had my doubts."

"And you also had a great need to share your concerns with us. Over and over again," I giggled.

John raised his arms in appeasement. "I've already apologized. Phoenix is a winning horse. And we're a winning team."

"Yes, we are," I replied, smiling.

"To celebrate the day, we can grill steaks, a recommendation from Sophia, or we can go straight to the marshmallows that Elli recommended," John suggested.

"We've been so good, we've earned dessert right away," I answered, grinning.

"Good choice."

John fetched a bag of marshmallows, two sharpened sticks, and a blanket from the car, then we sat down by the campfire and roasted marshmallows.

"I love marshmallows," I sighed contentedly as I licked my sticky fingers. "Even if they lead to a medium-level stickiness massacre."

John took my hand and sucked on one finger after another. "I'm happy to help clean up this massacre."

I giggled. While I continued to roast marshmallows, John and I talked about how he had managed to do all this within a few hours.

"Sophia and Elli really didn't tell you anything?" John asked, amazed.

I shook my head. "No. They didn't say a word, even though their behavior was pretty conspicuous."

"Interesting. Normally, those two can't keep such secrets to themselves for a minute."

"So there's hope," I joked.

We grinned at each other. While John used a branch to push the logs into embers, I stared thoughtfully into the flames. I felt like I was in a fairy tale.

I was in the most beautiful place in the world, cuddling with my dream prince, and we were eating marshmallows.

"It's really beautiful here," I said dreamily.

"You make this place special for me," John murmured, and I kissed him. Every time our lips touched, butterflies danced in my stomach and my heart beat wildly.

When we parted, John looked at me questioningly.

"Do you like being in New York?"

"Hm. I think so," I answered, shrugging. "Why?"

"Because you never talk about the city. No matter who you're talking to about it, you always change the subject."

"New York can't be described, it has to be experienced," I answered, smiling and hoping that John wouldn't ask any more questions. But I knew exactly what he was getting at, and I was afraid of it.

"You've been here for weeks without making a single phone call to New York."

I flinched when John caught me. I hadn't lied, but I had withheld a large part of the truth from him.

"My business manages fine without me," I answered, sighing. It was the truth. My - run-into-the-ground - business could do well without me. All of New York could!

"I've wanted to ask you for a long time why you really came back. But there was never the right moment."

There's never the right moment for questions like this.

I didn't know how to handle the tap-dancing elephant in the room finally being addressed.

Was I ready to speak the truth?

No, probably not...

"You know that. I had to take care of my grandparents' inheritance," I answered quickly.

"June." John looked at me reproachfully. "Why did you run away from New York?"

"I didn't run away!" I protested.

"What happened then?"

I thought long and hard about how to answer that.

"I turned my back on New York," I said quietly.

John lifted my chin and forced me to look him in the eyes. "Tell me what happened."

Sighing, I decided to face the elephant so it would finally disappear. "You were right, I fled New York because I don't have a job anymore."

John narrowed his eyes. "But you were a successful interior designer. It's obvious you have talent."

"That's true. But as it turns out now, my business partner didn't have a good handle on the finances. He ran our company into the ground. At full speed, without seatbelts or airbags."

"Why didn't you talk to me about this earlier? It must have been crushing you, right?" John asked.

I shrugged again. "I didn't want to destroy the image everyone had of me. If I had known from the start that I'd be staying here so long, maybe I wouldn't have built up this *everything-is-fine facade*. Finally saying it out loud really feels good."

John smiled at me gently.

"Is there anything else you want to talk about?"

I furrowed my brow thoughtfully. "Yes. When I found out that Frank - my partner - had run the company into the ground, I was relieved. Does that sound stupid?"

A tear rolled down my cheek and John wiped it away with his thumb.

"No, it doesn't," he answered.

"Of course it was terrible that almost all my money was gone, but I also had no more obligations. I hated my job. I had for a long time, I just didn't want to admit it to myself."

Saying out loud what I had felt for years felt good. A ton of weight lifted from my shoulders.

"And what did you want to do instead?"

I stretched out my arms. "This. Create a real home."

"Then you now have the chance for a fresh start," John said.

"Yes." I wiped another tear from my face. I didn't know exactly why I was even crying, because there was no reason for it. "Thank you for listening to me."

John hugged me and kissed my forehead. Then I stuffed another marshmallow into my mouth and buried my turbulent feelings in what felt like a ton of caramelized sugar foam.

For the first time in years, I felt like everything was okay. There were no more problems, no suppressed feelings, no broken heart, no loneliness, nothing that could cloud my joy. There was only John, me, and the paradise around us.

"I wish this moment would never end," I sighed.

"Unfortunately, that's not how life works. But we could repeat this moment. Again and again."

"If only it were that simple," I replied, smiling at him.

John looked at me seriously and I lost myself in his hazel eyes.

"It is simple. Stay here with me," he said with conviction.

My heart skipped a beat.

Chapter 16 – John

I steered the truck into the yard. When I saw Elli, Sophia, and June in the round pen, I had to smile. The three were as inseparable as ever. I quickly jumped out of the vehicle, brushed the last sawdust from my clothes, and ran to the women. Just one or two more days and the holiday ranch would be finished. Finally. The last few weeks had been exhausting, but they had been worth it. In two weeks, the first guests would arrive, and the houses were already booked until late autumn.

Prime Tribute, one of Rachel's horses, was standing with the girls in the round pen.

When June saw me, she waved at me with a smile. In the past, she would have climbed over the fence and almost knocked me over with enthusiasm. But for the past few days, June had been holding back. More precisely, since the night I had asked her to stay. I walked over to her.

I would have loved to grab her by the hips, pull her up, and kiss her passionately. Instead, I settled for a kiss on the cheek.

My sisters greeted me the same way.

"Hey," said June. She avoided my gaze.

"Hey," I replied. "I missed you."

She smiled at me but said nothing.

Damn, this couldn't go on like this, or I'd lose my mind. June's distance was driving me crazy. And I had no clue why she was doing it.

"How are you getting on?" I asked, trying to break the uncomfortable silence.

"I think today we can make a new attempt to get Prime Tribute used to another horse," said Elli, looking optimistically at the black horse.

Sophia stroked Prime Tribute's neck. "Should I get Penny?"

Elli nodded. "Let's try it."

"Do you think that's a good idea?" I asked critically. "I've never seen you flee over fences so often."

My little sister rolled her eyes with a snort.

"That's old news," Elli waved off. "Penny is the sweetest horse in the world. She'll charm Prime Tribute for sure."

"If you say so," I grumbled.

Sophia climbed over the fence as June's phone vibrated. She rejected the call without looking at the display.

Elli eyed June's smartphone critically. "Man, someone's persistent. You should answer it."

"Ah, it's nothing. Just an annoying telemarketer," June brushed it off. Her voice trembled and I could read the uncertainty on her face.

"June?" I asked, looking at her seriously. "What's going on?"

"Nothing!" June replied, agitated. Startled by her volume, she flinched and cleared her throat. "I'll help Sophia with Penny."

June also climbed over the fence.

I watched her go but didn't follow, only growling softly.

"Could you please check if Nougat is still in her stall?" Elli called after them, and June nodded.

"You still haven't found a place for the goat?" I asked, surprised.

Since the goat had appeared out of nowhere, she kept escaping from Elli. Sometimes we found her in the hayloft, sometimes by the river on the west pasture. No matter how escape-proof the stalls were, Nougat found a way out.

"No, not yet. But I hope that will change soon. Nougat is turning everything upside down."

Elli giggled. Then she cast a worried glance towards the stable.

"You should check on June and Sophia, they're taking quite a while."

"Hm, I'd rather wait here," I replied.

"Oh, oh. Trouble in paradise?" Elli looked at me with a frown.

I shrugged. "Good question."

"You've been acting strange for a few days now. What happened?"

"I'd like to know that too."

Elli threw Prime Tribute's lead rope around his neck and walked towards me.

"You did something stupid, didn't you, big brother?"

I sighed. "No. If anything, it's June who's acting weird. Since I suggested she stay here..."

Elli looked at me excitedly. "You asked her if she wants to stay here? Here at *Red Rivers*?"

"Yes. At the campfire, when we were celebrating our victory. I thought she had told you about it."

Elli shook her head in disbelief. "What were you thinking?"

To be honest, I didn't understand my sister's reaction at all.

"The real question is: Why hasn't June answered me to this day."

"Because that's not a question you can answer right away."

"I wanted her not to run away from me again. She's much happier here than in New York."

Now Elli gave me a pitying look, as if I were an old, sick dog. "That's sweet. But put yourself in her shoes. You're perfect together, but you've only been back together for a few weeks. You can't expect her to give up her whole life for you right away."

"I would drop everything for her," I answered bitterly.

"And June will do that for you too. But we women need more time to listen to our hearts. Give June that time; if you push her, you might regret it forever."

"Why are you so complicated?" I asked.

"Why are you so insensitive?" Elli countered with a grin.

Before June and Sophia came out of the stable with Penny, Rachel's red sports car raced across the yard.

Damn it!

Why did problems always come in packs?

Rachel got out of her luxury car with a flourish and came towards us, beaming.

"Hello there," she greeted us. "I wanted to see how everything's going."

"Things are going great with Golden Magic, you saw him jump yesterday," Elli evaded.

"And what about Prime Tribute?" Rachel asked, leaning against the fence.

"We're making small progress," Elli answered with a smile.

"Very good." Rachel put her hands on her hips. "How are you, John? You're hardly ever seen at *Red Rivers* anymore."

Rachel threw her arms around my neck, and I slowly but firmly pushed her away.

"There's a lot to do at the holiday ranch," I replied.

"You absolutely must show me your sweet project sometime." Rachel grinned at me.

"As soon as June is finished with everything, we'd be happy to show you around." I emphasized June's name in particular. I hated having to remain friendly with Rachel.

We still relied on Rachel's payment. For now. I could hardly wait to finally get rid of her. I wasn't an idiot. Rachel had only rediscovered her interest in me after June showed up. She had already destroyed our relationship once; I couldn't let it happen a second time.

"It's really nice that you check on your horses every day, but you don't have to. They're in good hands with me," said Elli. She suppressed a sigh and smiled at Rachel. My sister was an expert in her field, but she hated being watched while working.

"Of course. I'm paying you good money, so I want to see progress."

"And we're making it," Elli replied confidently, looking towards the horse stable.

Sophia led the saddled Penny out of the stable, followed by June, whose expression had frozen even before she saw Rachel.

My sister immediately switched gears. "Oh Rachel. Good to see you. We have something to discuss," Sophia said. She winked at me, then pressed Penny's reins into June's hand.

"Hey Sophia. Sure, what's up?"

"Let's discuss this on the porch. You need to sign some documents."

"Okay," Rachel said, displeased. But she followed Sophia to the main house.

When Sophia turned around briefly, I mouthed a silent *thank you*.

"Well, I guess the work falls to us then," Elli sighed and grinned at June, who hadn't said anything yet.

"Looks like it." A forced smile played on her lips, which I saw through immediately. Something was weighing on her mind, and I wanted to know what it was. More than that, I wanted to take the burden off her shoulders, but I didn't know how.

"Ready?" Elli asked.

"Ready," June replied.

"Nobody's asking me, but I still think this is a bad idea," I said thoughtfully. "That horse is dangerous."

"You're right, nobody's asking you," Elli retorted.

June mounted the saddle, and I reluctantly opened the gate to the round pen.

There were a good ten meters between Prime Tribute and Penny.

"Tell me when I should come closer," June said, waiting in the saddle for further instructions. Elli, who was speaking soothingly to Prime Tribute, nodded, and Penny took a step closer.

I watched June with eagle eyes. She was riding straight towards an unpredictable horse, and I was worried about her.

When they were only five meters apart, I relaxed a bit. Prime Tribute had his ears pricked, but he remained standing calmly.

"This is going great," June cheered.

"Oh yes. You're doing really well," Elli praised the black horse and patted his neck.

"See, John. It's not so bad," June said and smiled at me. My heart soared and I smiled back.

Elli nodded to June. "I think we can take one more step."

"Okay." June clicked her tongue and let Penny take another step forward.

My sister had good intuition, not just with horses. I stood next to Penny and placed my hand on June's thigh.

"I'm sorry I pressured you into making a decision," I murmured.

June looked at me, puzzled. "What?"

"You know," I sighed.

"No," June replied.

"You've been acting strange for days."

June adjusted her cowboy hat, using it as an excuse to avoid looking me in the face any longer.

"What happened between us?" I asked.

"Please, let's talk about this later."

No. I couldn't stand the tension between us for another second. Whatever had gone wrong between us, we needed to sort it out, and right now.

"You're running away," I growled.

"I'm right here," June answered. Then she glanced at Rachel. "We'll talk about everything when we're alone."

"Okay." A compromise was better than nothing.

Things were going so well with Prime Tribute that Elli decided to come one step closer.

Everything was fine until June's phone vibrated and she became restless. Her unease transferred to Penny, who took two more steps forward - Suddenly Prime Tribute broke free from Elli's lead rope and reared up, whinnying. Penny pinned her ears back and nervously pranced back and forth.

"Whoa," Elli tried to calm the rearing stallion, while June tried to stay in the saddle.

I wanted to grab Penny's reins, but I was too slow. She made two bucks and threw June off, who hit the ground hard.

My damn heart stopped when she lay motionless on the ground.

"Get this monster out of here!" I barked at Elli. She reacted immediately by closing the gate and taking cover while Prime Tribute carried on in the round pen like a rabid beast.

I immediately ran to June, who was lying face down, and turned her over.

"June? Are you okay?"

Carefully, I brushed her brown hair out of her face. No wounds. Good!

June opened her eyes, looking confused, and I exhaled in relief. Never in my entire life had I been as scared as I was in that moment.

I glared daggers at Prime Tribute. That damn beast could have killed her!

"Are you alright?" I asked.

When June realized she had fallen, she flailed her arms wildly and staggered to her feet.

"I'm fine," she said, dusting off her clothes.

"Are you sure?" I took her chin between my thumb and forefinger, forcing her to look at me. "That fall looked dangerous."

"Everything's fine," June replied, annoyed. "It's not the first time I've fallen, and it certainly won't be the last."

Sophia, who had caught Penny, cautiously approached. "Is everything okay?"

June nodded. "Perfectly fine!"

Rachel, standing right next to Sophia, scrutinized us critically. "Looks like Prime Tribute still needs a lot of small improvements before he can come back to us."

Elli ran her hand through her hair nervously. "It wasn't his fault. We got distracted."

June sighed. "It won't happen again. Believe me, I'm this close to setting my phone on fire."

June being so emotional and angry was unlike her. Was this really about our conversation from a few days ago? To be honest, I couldn't imagine it. Yes, she hadn't responded to me, but she had only started this strange behavior the next morning.

I stroked June's upper arm. "We should still take you to the doc in Merryville, just to be safe."

She swatted my arm away. "I don't need a doctor, just some rest."

It was happening again. June was running away from me.

She left me standing there like an idiot in the rain while she ran towards the paddocks. I wanted to run after her, to spank her damn ass and ask her what had gotten into her. It couldn't be that we were forever doomed to June fleeing from me and me letting her go.

I wanted to follow her, but Elli's look stopped me.

"Give her five minutes."

Okay, I'd give her five minutes, but not a second more. And if I had to put June over my knee in front of everyone to finally get her to say what was wrong, I'd do it.

Chapter 17 – June

After leaving *Red Rivers* behind, I pulled my smartphone out of my pocket. It hadn't stopped ringing for days, which made me want to throw it in the river. But part of me was curious about Frank's request. My head was pounding like hell, but it was no longer due to the fall.

I had sworn not to exchange another word with my former business partner, but the issue wasn't entirely settled for me either.

Frank's calls showed that the perfect world I was living in was just a fantasy, and I hated this realization. Frank had burst the bubble. For that alone, he deserved all my anger. Instead, I had taken it out on John.

Oh, John...

He had blamed himself, I had seen and felt that. I should have told him, but I couldn't. Saying it out loud hurt too much. New York had caught up with me.

My phone buzzed again. Frank Austin's name appeared on the glowing display once more. But this time, I didn't reject the caller.

"What is it?" I asked, trying to sound as indifferent as possible.

"June, for God's sake, I finally reached you!" He sounded agitated, but I wasn't impressed. Frank had a talent for sweeping others along. That's the only reason I had become his partner.

"I hope it's important. Thanks to you, I just fell off a horse."

"Oh." My fall only briefly slowed his enthusiasm. "What are you still doing in that backwater town?"

I should have hung up just for how contemptuously he said the word *backwater*. But I wasn't going to let him off that easily. I wanted to rub it in his face that he was to blame for everything.

"I'm still in Merryville because I lost everything in New York. Thanks to you."

"I miscalculated. It happens," Frank tried to appease me.

What a massive ass. He was the asshole of the millennium!

"You ruined us both!" I yelled into the phone. Now I couldn't hold back my anger and tears anymore.

"And now I'm saving both our asses!"

I paused. "What do you mean by that?"

"I have an investor who might be able to save us. He owns a hotel chain that needs a complete overhaul. But you need to come back to New York, immediately."

"You can't expect me to drop everything for a *maybe*."

"Come on, June. It's New York! What do you have to lose in Merryville?"

"My life," I replied and hung up.

Who did Frank think he was, barging into my life and complicating everything? A few days ago, everything had been so simple. My life in New York was in the past, and my new life in Merryville had begun.

Okay, it hadn't been that simple. When John had asked me to stay by the campfire a few days ago, I couldn't answer. I was paralyzed. Of course, my heart had screamed *yes*, but my mind had hesitated. I had only wanted to sleep on it for a night before agreeing, but then Frank had started bombarding me with calls. These calls had sown doubts that were taking root. Until now. Now I could finally close the chapter on New York.

I turned around and let my gaze sweep over *Red Rivers'* houses and barns. This was home. This was my family. This was where my heart lived.

How could Frank expect me to give all this up at the snap of a finger?

My phone vibrated. This time it wasn't a call, but a message.

Think about it. But think fast, you only have a few days.

Now he wasn't just making demands, but demands with an ultimatum.

I was so angry that I threw my smartphone as far as I could. It felt good to vent my anger. Until I realized what I had done.

Shocked, I ran to where I thought my phone might be, got down on my knees, and searched the ground. The tall grass was a real problem.

"I like seeing you on your knees," John said, suddenly standing behind me. "But for my taste, you're still wearing too much."

I quickly wiped my cheeks with my sleeve to dry my tears.

"You're an idiot. Better help me search," I replied seriously. John looked at me grinning, and even though I fought against it, I smiled. I was infinitely grateful that John wasn't angry with me because of my outburst. Then I cleared my throat while continuing to feel the ground. "I mean it. Help me look!"

"What are you looking for?" John asked, crouching down.

"My smartphone. I threw it away," I answered with a sigh.

John raised an eyebrow questioningly and put a hand on my forehead. "Are you sure I shouldn't take you to Dr. Duke after all?"

An angry look from me was enough, and John helped me search for my phone.

"Why did you throw it away?"

"Because I was angry."

"Because of the fall?"

John looked at me critically. I knew I would have to endure these looks for a while longer. Until he could be sure that I hadn't seriously injured myself in the fall.

Heavens, I was completely out of it. I was blaming the man who loved me for caring about me. This couldn't go on. I had tried to keep New York away from us for the past few days, which had led to me keeping John away from me.

"It's not because of the fall, it's because of the reason why I fell," I sighed.

"The phone call?"

I nodded.

"I assume it wasn't a pleasant conversation if you threw your phone into the paddock afterwards," John said.

"No, it was awful," I sobbed.

John took me in his arms and stroked the back of my head comfortingly. I pressed myself tightly against his chest and breathed in his scent. He smelled of cedar wood and hay, he smelled like home.

"Do you want to talk about it?" John asked.

No, I didn't want to. But I had to.

"It was my former partner." John looked at me questioningly and I nodded. "Yes, exactly. The one who ruined everything."

"And what did he want?" His jaw muscles tensed. If Frank were here now, John would have punched him, and I wouldn't have stopped him.

"For me to come back."

John growled, his serious gaze piercing me. "What did you say?"

"That I won't drop everything just because he wants me to."

A smile flitted across John's lips. "You refused?"

I bit my lower lip thoughtfully. "I think so."

"Good," John murmured and brushed a strand of hair from my face. "I wouldn't have let you go anyway."

Even though John said the perfect words, was the perfect gentleman, I started to sob.

With anger and confusion.

I broke away from John and jumped up. "What does that idiot think anyway? I should never have answered the call!"

John listened patiently as I vented my anger. When I had calmed down, I looked at John questioningly.

"Was it right to refuse?"

John rubbed his chin thoughtfully. "What does your gut tell you?"

I answered without hesitation: "Yes, it was right."

"Then it was right to refuse." John smiled at me and I loved him for letting me decide whether it was right or wrong.

I snuggled against his strong chest, let his strong arms wrap around me, and kissed him. His rough stubble rubbed against my skin and his masculine scent enveloped me.

We parted and resumed our search for my phone.

"What will we do when we find your phone?"

I glanced at the afternoon sun and thought. My mood was still at rock bottom. So I shrugged. "No idea."

"Insiders have told me that *Ben & Jerry's* can solve any problem."

I giggled softly. "Your insiders told you that?"

"Yes. And they also told me that there's a seemingly endless supply in the freezer."

"Three cheers for your insiders who so generously share information and ice cream with you," I said, smiling.

"Oh, they won't share the ice cream willingly. There's even a chance there will be a fight to the death."

My smile turned into loud laughter.

It was sweet of John to try to cheer me up, but my problem was at least a level five problem and ice cream had its limits at level four.

We resumed our search for my phone, and I hated myself for throwing it onto the densely overgrown paddock in my fit of rage. After what felt like an eternity on my knees, I finally saw something glittering in the grass.

"I've got it!" I cheered and crawled purposefully towards the light reflection.

Sobered, I realized that the display was cracked and had deep fissures.

"Damn it," I sighed. At least it still worked somewhat. The display lit up, even though part of it flickered like a distorted image.

John took the smartphone from my hand.

"It's not that bad," John said calmly.

"Not that bad? My phone is dying!"

"Then let it go," John replied, grinning. Then he looked at me again with that serious gaze that made my lower abdomen tingle. "What do you need it for anyway?"

I would have loved to throw at least ten reasons at him why I still needed my smartphone, but I couldn't even think of three arguments. John was right. The phone was part of my old New York life, and that had obviously developed cracks.

Without addressing his question, I took my phone back and said, "I know what we're going to do."

My heart was ready to leave New York behind and start anew here. But I wasn't ready to say it out loud yet.

"Will I have to engage in a heroic battle for my lady?" John struck a heroic pose and flexed his biceps.

"No," I giggled. "I don't need a knight in shining armor. I need a cowboy who knows how to handle his lasso."

"I like that. Tell me more about it," John murmured.

"I'm ready. For anything you have in mind for me."

I meant that seriously.

John's eyes flashed darkly. "You have no idea how dangerous such an offer is."

"Yes, I do. But I trust you. And I trust that you'll help me forget this terrible day."

"Nothing I'd like more," John murmured.

The drive to the holiday ranch took longer than I would have liked. I was excited because I didn't know what to expect. But my lower abdomen was tingling mightily. Judging by John's look, he already knew exactly what he wanted to do with me. I hoped he would fuck my brains out so I could forget everything that had happened so far today.

So much chaos, so many emotions, and so few ways to sort it all out.

What did fate have against me?

If my life were a book, I would have wished for the campfire to be our last chapter, ending with the sentence *And they lived happily ever after*. But life didn't grant either me or John a happy ending. At least not yet; we needed a little more patience. If we had to while away the waiting time in our special vacation cabin, that wasn't the worst thing that could happen to us.

I smiled at the thought of *our* vacation cabin. It was the first one to be finished, and John had equipped it with some upgrades that I was gradually getting to know. I would have loved to live there forever. But how high were the chances of that happening? How likely was it that our story would end right there?

"What do you have planned for me?" I asked curiously. I liked it when John whispered to me how he wanted to drive me out of my mind.

"A gentleman keeps quiet and enjoys," John replied.

"You're a cowboy," I corrected him.

"An old-school cowboy," John countered with a grin.

"Okay, you win. Then keep me in suspense," I sighed, grinning.

"That's exactly what I intend to do," he murmured. "And I won't let you go before the next sunrise."

I smiled at him and examined his hazel eyes, which were focused on the road. John had last shaved two days ago, and I loved the rough, dark stubble that covered his face. It made him look so mysterious and masculine.

Arriving at the ranch, John wasted no time. He closed the door behind us and looked at me expectantly.

"Take off your clothes and kneel in front of me on the floor." His dominant voice echoed through the room.

I complied with his wish and undressed without breaking eye contact. His pupils dilated as I let my bra fall to the floor, and he growled softly. Lastly, I took off my panties, then knelt in front of John. From this perspective, he looked even taller than he already was.

He walked around me and examined me critically. Every time John looked at me like this, it took my breath away.

Heavens, I love these looks!

"Put your hands behind your back," he murmured. I obeyed, placing my hands behind my back and grasping my forearms with my hands.

"I love it when you kneel before me like this, baby."

John rubbed his stubble, which nearly drove me crazy, and continued to observe me.

"Who do you belong to?" he asked.

"I belong to you," I answered.

"That's right, baby. You belong only to me and no one else."

"I belong only to you," I repeated his words.

Forever.

John smiled contentedly and opened his jeans.

Eagerly, I watched as his magnificent erection sprang free.

Without saying a word, he grabbed my hair and pushed me towards his hips. I opened my mouth and let his manhood slide into me. Now John really had control over me, and I gladly surrendered it to him. I trusted him. He knew exactly where my boundaries were, even better than I did myself.

John also grabbed my hair with his other hand and guided my head while his hips kept coming closer to me. His erection slid deeper into my throat with each thrust. Still, I kept looking into John's eyes.

"I don't want you to doubt that you belong here," he panted.

I couldn't answer, but he didn't expect an answer either.

John thrust even deeper.

"I don't want you to leave, damn it. I want you to stay here."

Now he pushed his manhood all the way into my throat and held still. He didn't take his eyes off me. The hazel of his irises was consumed by the black of his pupils and flashed darkly.

It was challenging, but my entire body trembled with arousal. This kind of humiliation excited me even more in real life than in my fantasies.

"Your place is at Red Rivers, by my side," John continued.

Slowly, I was running out of air; I tried to relax and closed my eyes. Immediately, John placed a hand on my cheek. Still, his grip was so firm that I couldn't move my head.

"Keep looking at me, baby."

I opened my eyes again and looked at him with pleading glances. John responded with a grin that said how much he was enjoying the situation.

Me, naked kneeling on the floor, with his hard erection deep in my throat and a submissive, pleading look.

"Your place is by my side... and sometimes in front of me, on your knees."

That was the most beautiful declaration of love a man could make to me, and I knew John was right. My place was right here, and we were on the verge of *And they lived happily ever after*.

John looked at me for endless long seconds before releasing my head so I could catch my breath. I took a deep breath, wanting to tell John that I wanted to stay with him. That I had long since written off New York. My life in New York was a lie that had developed such deep cracks that everyone could see the truth underneath.

"I..." I began. But John put his finger on my lips and interrupted me.

"No, June. I don't want you to answer now, but when the ecstasy is over."

I closed my mouth and nodded.

"You belong to me. I'm going to make you forget everything else now, because nothing else matters."

John closed his pants and then held out his hand to me. I took it and stood up.

"Close your eyes and stretch out your arms!" he commanded in a gentle voice.

I closed my eyes and breathed as shallowly as I could to hear every sound. He opened a drawer and took something out.

"I love ropes. Depending on their composition, they can caress the skin gently or be a real punishment," John said. He tied something cool around my wrists that nestled softly against my skin. It was a real, old-fashioned lasso made of leather, not synthetic fiber.

The material felt so beautiful that I wanted to wear it forever. A clearly visible sign for everyone that I belonged to John.

My eyes were still closed when John stood in front of me, guided my arms upward, and fixed them above my head.

"You're going to hate me for this position soon, but I want you to endure it for me anyway."

I bit my lip thoughtfully, because I felt comfortable. My body was relaxed, the leather restraints even gave me support.

John took my earlobe between his teeth and licked it.

"Don't worry, baby. You'll understand what I mean soon," he whispered in my ear.

Then came a jerk and I was pulled up by the lasso so far that only my tiptoes touched the ground.

John took my chin between his thumb and forefinger. "Look at me, baby!"

Blinking to adjust to the light, I opened my eyes. John's dominant gaze made my legs weak. If I hadn't been hanging from the ceiling, I would have simply fallen over.

"What do you think I'm going to do with you now?" he asked. His hands roamed over my body. He grabbed my hips and pressed my pubic area against his hard erection.

"I don't know," I answered.

"Wrong answer." John smiled seductively at me. "I'm going to do whatever I please with you."

John went back to the drawer and brought out a handful of wooden clothespins.

When he placed the first clip on the inside of my upper arm, I took a quick breath. But to my surprise, I found that the clip hurt much less than I had thought. Several more clips lined up on my upper arm, then John turned his attention to the other arm.

The light, pulsing pressure grew slightly with each heartbeat, just like my desire.

John also placed some clips on my breasts. He repeatedly ran his fingers over the clips, flicked them, or bent them to the side. This elicited a soft moan from me. These clips really had very narrow boundaries between pleasure and pain.

Growling softly, John walked around me and looked at me. His hand wandered between my legs and I moaned. He rubbed my clit and I tilted my head back to enjoy his touch.

"What should I do with you next?" John asked. He kept rubbing my most sensitive spot.

"Is that all with the clips?" I asked teasingly. His gaze darkened.

"You want more?" John growled. "No problem, baby. But don't say later that I didn't warn you."

John went around me and got more clips and strings. Curiously, I watched what he was planning to do with them.

John attached the first clip to my side, making sure that the thin string lay between my skin and the clip. I gasped loudly. I wasn't prepared for such intense pain. The skin over my ribs was much more sensitive than on my arms. And with each breath, the clip felt like it would slip off at any moment.

"What are the strings for?" I asked, panting.

John smiled knowingly. "So I can pull off the clips with one tug. There's no more beautiful pain and no more beautiful screams."

To illustrate his point, he pulled on the string, which made me bite my lips to hide the pain. If John believed I could endure the pain, then I could endure it.

Nevertheless, my heart began to beat wildly and I felt the clips more and more distinctly. John mercilessly continued to cover my flanks with clips. But the stronger the pain throbbed, the hotter my lower body became. I could even still feel John's hands between my legs, so intense were all the sensations.

John took two more clips from the drawer and connected them with a metal key chain. I guessed what they were meant for, and John's grin confirmed my suspicions.

"Take a deep breath!"

I followed John's command, whereupon he attached the clips to my buds.

The little things triggered the second most intense sensations I had ever experienced.

John pulled on the chain, forcing me to take half a step towards him on my tiptoes, which completely exhausted my range of motion. He licked my lower lip until I opened my mouth. Growling, he entered and our tongues met. My whole body caught fire as sparks flew between us.

"Please," I whispered. I couldn't say more because it was hard for me to form a clear thought. I was overstimulated with pain, lust, and the deep feelings I had for John. "I want you."

"I know. But you have to be patient a little longer."

Grinning, John pulled on the chain even harder. Now I couldn't take another step forward. I returned John's gaze. He expected me to beg him to stop. For that reason alone, I bit my lips. Yes, the pain was intense, but my pride was greater!

Once again, John let his hands wander over the clips. Each of his touches triggered tremors inside me. John was pouring gasoline on the fire. And if he didn't throw me on the bed and take me right now, I would burn up.

John paused at a clip on my upper arm and removed it. Reflexively, I wanted to fall to my knees in pain, but the restraints prevented me from doing so.

Only when I managed to calm my breathing did the pain subside.

Oh. My. God.

Dozens of clamps were still hanging on my body! How was I supposed to endure this?

John stroked the reddened area where the clamp had been. Even his gentle touch burned like fire. Then he removed two more clamps, taking my breath away.

"Trust me, the remaining clamps will give you more pleasure," John murmured.

More pleasure? He was the only one enjoying the clamps right now! But I didn't say a word and trusted that John was right.

His hand slid between my legs. Despite... or because of the pain, I had become even wetter, and my lower body yearned for release.

Two of his fingers entered me. It wasn't the release I longed for, but it eased my hunger.

John removed the next clamp from my arm. Now that John was inside me, the pain felt different. Much less intense. Instead, I felt his fingers so clearly inside me that I almost came.

I looked at John in amazement. Every day with John was a gift, and every night with him was a revelation.

"You see, baby," he said, planting a soft kiss on my lips. "I'm leading you to paradise."

I nodded and smiled at him. "But it's unfair that I have to go through hell first."

"No. That's not unfair, it's a big part of the fun."

Admittedly, John was right. As painful as the clamps were, I had never been so aroused in my entire life. Although I was tied up, I felt safe and secure.

When I didn't respond, John forced me to look at him. "You like it, don't you?"

He looked at me seriously, but I could see from his expression that he already knew my answer. John had seen right through me. Me and the deep desires within me that I didn't even know existed.

"Yes, I like it very much," I said.

John walked around me. He examined me again, and I loved his gaze.

"And you'll love it more each time. You'll long to kneel before me. You'll crave the clamps, the strikes, the chance to serve me."

His voice was rough and husky, like a hungry wolf, and his words ignited a huge fire in my lower body that eclipsed all other sensations.

John removed all the clamps that weren't connected to the rope while he let me come for the first time.

The fire in my lower body exploded with such a loud bang that I briefly blacked out. Breathing heavily, I hung in the restraints, waiting for John to untie me.

When he didn't untie me, I opened my eyes and looked at him questioningly.

"We're far from finished. I promised I'd fuck you until dawn."

I moaned softly, wondering how many orgasms of this kind I could endure. As it looked, John had committed himself to getting to the bottom of this question.

He played with the clamps, and I squirmed under his touch. But I didn't have much room to move. I could only turn to the side, which led John to simply switch sides where he made me feel the clamps.

He loosened some clamps for half a second, which was enough to take my breath away. Other clamps he pressed even tighter, making me inhale sharply. John managed to control not only my breath with these small, wooden things, but also my desire. And with his brown eyes, his rough voice, and that well-toned body, John controlled my heart.

Slowly he unbuttoned his shirt, and my pulse shot up. His upper body was flawless, his tanned skin stretched tightly over his muscles. I wanted to caress the contours of his rock-hard six-pack and then follow the hair that started at his navel and wandered down to his erection.

Just thinking about it, I could feel myself getting wetter. John was driving me crazy!

John saw my greedy look. "You want more of that?"

"Oh yes." I licked my lips and waited to be allowed to see more of John.

He opened his pants again, and I could feel the relief even before he let his erection slide between my legs.

He rubbed against my pearl, and I could already feel the next orgasm approaching. John grabbed my thighs, lifted me up, and entered me while I wrapped my legs around his hips.

I moaned loudly as his erection slid into me to the hilt. It was pure relief and at the same time fueled my desire for more. I tilted my pelvis as far as I could and circled my hips while John thrust into me again and again.

My walls tightened around his hardness, my G-spot becoming the center of the fire.

John's eyes grew darker, his panting more guttural, and his thrusts harder. I liked it when he took what he wanted. I adored his dominance.

"Hold on tight, baby," John groaned, grinning. Then he grinned as he pulled on the string on my left side. He yanked it, and the clamps flew off in all directions.

I screamed, my whole body trembling, and the pain seamlessly transitioned into my next orgasm.

"What are you doing to me?" I asked breathlessly.

"I'm making you feel things no one else can evoke in you," John replied.

He continued to take me, and his endurance seemed endless. His trained chest glistened, and I watched as his muscles tensed every second.

John's body was truly worship-worthy! So toned and defined. I felt safe with him because I knew he could protect me from anything that might be dangerous.

The third orgasm overtook me, and I was officially addicted to more.

I was addicted to John.

I was addicted to what he was doing to me.

And I was addicted to what it triggered inside me.

This fiery tingling that shot through my entire body from my core was incredible. Even after three orgasms, I wasn't done. I wanted another orgasm. Or two. Maybe I even wanted to sleep with John all night long.

"You still want more?" John asked, amazed.

"Yes," I moaned. "Please!"

His eyes lit up with excitement.

"Damn, I love how hot you are."

"I want another orgasm," I panted.

John grinned at me. "You'll get your orgasm."

Judging by his smile, there was a *but* coming, and I hoped it would only be a tiny *but*.

"But you'll have to do something for me." He thrust hard one more time, then pulled out of me, and I looked down longingly at his erection.

"What do I have to do?" I asked.

"You're going to release the last clamps yourself."

Since John had withdrawn from me, the clamps on my right side were throbbing and burning with each heartbeat. And my heart was beating pretty fast. Just the thought of having to remove the clamps myself sent a shiver down my spine. Without restraints, I wouldn't have been able to handle a single clamp. And without John inside me, certainly not!

"I don't think I can do it," I sighed, saying goodbye to my fourth orgasm.

"You can," John said firmly. "But I'll leave the decision up to you whether you will or not."

Then he took the loose end of the rope attached to the topmost clamp in one hand and my ankle in the other. He lifted my heel towards my butt, and I briefly lost my balance. Even when both my feet were on the ground, the position had been torture because only my toes had touched the floor. Now, with just one leg, I swayed precariously back and forth.

John tied the rope to my ankle.

"This is your definition of free choice?" I asked, unable to avoid a defiant tone.

John smiled at me. "Yes. It's your decision whether you move your leg or not."

I daggers at John with my eyes and concentrated on maintaining my balance. To do so, I tilted my head back and took a deep breath.

"How long do I have to decide?" I asked.

"That's for me to decide," John answered softly. I felt his gaze on me, as gentle as his voice. Both, combined with the dominance, drove me crazy.

Even though what John was doing hurt... I still liked it. Even now, my insides were quivering and tingling with desire.

With each passing second, my leg grew heavier, and I felt the topmost clothespin slipping further. I held my breath and tried to keep controlling my body, but it became increasingly difficult. My pulse was racing, yet it felt like hours passed between heartbeats.

"I love your stubbornness, June." John lovingly brushed a strand of my brown hair from my face. I smiled, enjoying his fingers on my skin.

Then his other hand spread my legs, briefly throwing me off balance. The topmost clamp flew off, and I had to suppress a cry before regaining my composure.

"I could be fucking you again by now," John murmured.

He gave me a taste of what I wanted.

It would have been smarter to give up my rebellion, but I couldn't. Not with that look, not with those words! I wanted to show him what I was made of, so I took a deep breath.

"Can't you take it anymore?" I asked, smiling bravely.

"Damn, baby. You're really asking for it, aren't you?" He looked at me darkly.

"I can and I will," I replied.

Then John grabbed me by the hips, spread my legs even wider, and entered me again. Finally! My burning side subsided, the tingling in my center reignited.

John thrust as hard as he could, again and again. Mercilessly, to the hilt.

"Thank you," I gasped, close to orgasm.

"You're welcome, darling."

John rested his head on my shoulder. His rough stubble left a tingling sensation on my skin, while his hot breath was followed by goosebumps.

My legs trembled more and more from exertion and lust equally.

It was no longer possible. No chance I could keep my leg bent any longer. I closed my eyes, took a deep breath, and let my leg fall.

The clamps flew in all directions as I escaped into my fourth orgasm - the most intense orgasm I had ever experienced.

John followed me into ecstasy, and I felt his erection grow even harder before he came inside me.

We stood like that for a moment to catch our breath, then John removed my restraints and carried me to the bed. My eyelids grew heavy, and I snuggled against John's muscular chest.

"I needed that," I whispered.

He put his arm around my shoulder and gave me a loving look. It reminded me of the most intense feeling I had ever experienced.

Back then, when I saw John's hazel eyes for the very first time.

Chapter 18 – John

I LEANED AGAINST THE counter and smiled at Sue.

"The same again for me," I said, then looked at Sophia. "And for you, sis?"

Sophia let her gaze wander over the cake display.

"I'll have the same again too," she answered with a grin.

Sue took care of our order with a smile while Sophia sipped her hot chocolate with whipped cream.

"I still can't believe how beautiful the vacation ranch has become."

Yesterday, we had finished the last of the construction work.

"Me neither. June has outdone herself."

June had furnished each cabin differently, but they were all beautiful. According to her, only a few small elements were missing, which were now in the form of several bags between Sophia, me, and a basket full of cherries. Grandma had insisted on making cherry juice for the harvest helpers before the upcoming harvest.

"You've contributed a big part too," Sophia said, pointing at me with her spoon. "The cabins are like something out of a picture book. And the string lights are fantastic!"

I nodded appreciatively at my sister. Sue set a plate of rhubarb pie in front of me, and I happily stuck my fork into the piece of cake. Sophia looked at me with pity while waiting for her second helping.

"What?" I asked.

"Nothing, nothing," Sophia waved off. Then she leaned forward and whispered: "I just feel sorry for the rhubarb because it can't decide whether it wants to be a fruit or a vegetable."

I grinned. "When rhubarb ends up on Sue's cake, it's clearly a fruit."

Sue winked at me as she set a plate with two pieces of apple crumble pie in front of Sophia. "Sophia, dear. You could really broaden your horizons and try my other cakes too. Then you'll see for yourself how good my rhubarb pie is."

"I can confirm that," I replied with a half-full mouth.

"And miss out on the taste experience of the world's best cake? No way! You know I'm very conservative in this regard."

"Conservative or not. You can't live on apple crumble pies and burgers with extra bacon alone," I answered, frowning.

"Yes, I can. You can see that," Sophia said sweetly and ate her cake with relish. "Besides, I'm not the only one who maintains traditions."

Sophia grinned at me, infecting Sue, who was shamelessly eavesdropping on our conversation while halfheartedly wiping the counter. "Old love never dies."

"You can't compare me and June to cake and burgers," I grumbled.

"Yes, I can. I'm forced to when you criticize my - for me optimal - lifestyle."

I nudged Sophia in the side. "You started it by railing against my rhubarb pie."

"Okay, you're right. I should broaden my horizons, but not now," Sophia replied, laughing.

"I'll do it later - the phrase of all great revolutionaries," I said dryly.

"I don't want to revolutionize anything," Sophia countered.

"Not with that attitude, you won't." I had to suppress my grin as Sophia snorted and rolled her eyes.

She ate her two large pieces faster than I ate my rhubarb pie.

"Speaking of revolution, have you asked June yet?" Sophia asked, pushing the last cake crumbs onto her fork. I looked at her, confused.

"What does my question have to do with revolution?"

"Actually, nothing. I just couldn't think of a better transition," Sophia said, shrugging.

"Next time, you'll nail it."

I patted my sister on the shoulder for her failed but cute attempt at not barging in Key-style.

"So, what's the deal?" Sophia pressed on.

"No, I haven't asked her yet."

"Why not?"

Well. Good question. Actually, everything between June and me was fine again, even more than fine, everything was going great. Subconsciously, I was afraid that my question would change something between us.

"The opportunity hasn't come up yet," I answered vaguely, hoping my sister would be satisfied with that. But Sophia was a true Key, of course that wasn't enough for her. She scooted closer to me and looked at me incredulously.

"You have to ask her! The sooner, the better."

"What difference does it make whether I ask her today or tomorrow? June is here, and she's not going to disappear anytime soon."

Sophia sighed. "It can make a very big difference."

"Is John planning to propose to June?" Sue asked, leaning over the counter with a hushed voice and a hungry look for sensation.

"Heavens, no," Sophia said, laughing. "It's about a job offer."

"Too bad," Sue replied and went to the other end of the counter.

"Don't you want to know what kind of job?" I called after Sue.

Sue waved it off. "No, but I want an invitation to the wedding when it finally happens."

Sophia giggled while I thought about when I should talk to June. Then my sister cleared her throat and looked at me seriously.

"Seriously, you need to ask June if she wants to take over the care of the vacation guests. Otherwise, we might as well shut down right away."

Sophia was right. Elli was fully occupied with the horses, Sophia took care of finances and organizing all important things all day, my brothers were busy planting and harvesting grain and vegetables, and I was tied up around the clock with repairs of fences and machinery.

Besides that, the holiday ranch felt like home to me. June and I had spent every free minute there. So why not just move in there, so the guests always had someone to talk to?

"You're right. I'll ask her as soon as I get back."

"Good. I'm sure she'll say *yes*. She loves the holiday ranch." Sophia tilted her head and looked at me dreamily. "And she loves you."

"I love her too," I replied.

Sophia looked at her watch. "Oh, I have to go. Grandma's waiting for the cherries. And after that, I can bring June the decorations."

I shook my head. "I'll bring her the decorations. I just need to load up Ellis's overpriced horse feed, then I'll follow."

"Okey-dokey." Sophia stood up and grabbed the basket full of cherries. "By the way, it's not overpriced horse feed, but high-quality premium mash. It's worth the price. Oh, and thanks for the cake." She left the diner grinning broadly, without looking back.

"You're welcome," I muttered and placed a twenty-dollar bill on the counter.

I left the diner to load Ellis's feed. This time there were only three bags, but they felt like they weighed three times what a hundredweight bag should weigh.

I was just loading the last of the three bags onto the truck bed when someone hugged me from behind. Strong perfume enveloped me, and I instantly knew who it was.

"Hey John. I didn't know how toned your upper body felt," she purred.

"Rachel," I growled and detached Rachel from me, who had been clinging to my chest.

I turned around and looked at her seriously. No one except June should get this close to me, it could be dangerous.

"What do you want?" I asked.

"To check on how my horse is doing," she answered with a smile. "Since I picked up Golden Magic, I haven't been to *Red Rivers*."

"It's going well," I lied. Since the first day Citizen Silver arrived, nothing had changed about his nature, even though Elli wished otherwise. Maybe there were just people, animals, situations that you couldn't change, no matter how much you wanted to.

Since June had been back in Merryville, I couldn't get rid of Rachel either.

"You've always known what you're doing." Rachel ran her finger across my chest.

"That's all Ellis's doing, she's the horse expert," I replied and pushed her hand aside.

"Don't be so modest," she said and pouted. "You know, John. You're a really great guy. So tall and strong and…"

"And taken," I interrupted Rachel.

"That didn't stop us last time." Rachel gave me a flutter of her eyelashes that she must have practiced for hours in front of the mirror.

"What's this about, Rachel?" I returned her eyelash flutter with a serious, unsympathetic look. My jaw muscles tensed and I had to restrain myself from reprimanding her.

Spoiled little brat! Rachel felt entitled to get what she wanted. Without regard for the consequences.

"I want you," Rachel said. "I want to find out what could have happened after our one and only kiss."

"But I don't. You'd better go now, before I forget myself," I threatened her. My threat was real. Damn, my blood was boiling and I really had to hold back.

I was a gentleman, no question, but even a gentleman sometimes lost control and vented his anger.

"Yes, I know, the *circumstances* aren't the best, but that's how it is," Rachel said in a soft voice. She was damn good at faking emotions. But I knew her well enough to know that these feelings were just an act. Rachel Pearson had no feelings, it was hereditary in her family. Feelings, inhibitions, and down-to-earthness didn't exist in the Pearsons' vocabulary.

"Why can't you just accept that June and I are together?" I asked.

"Because we belong together. Just give me one kiss, and I'll prove it to you."

I growled loudly and threateningly, but it didn't stop Rachel from coming even closer.

"Damn it, Rachel. Just stop it," I appealed to her reason one last time. "My heart belongs to June."

"Fine, believe that if you want. For now, I'll settle for the rest of your body," Rachel purred. Before I could react, her pink-painted lips were on mine.

Damn it all!

Chapter 19 – June

I SANG ALONG LOUDLY to Bonnie Buckley's latest hit blaring from the car radio as I turned onto the main road to Merryville. I loved Bonnie Buckley and I loved her music. To me, she was a national hero, and her songs were my anthems.

The arrow-straight road stretched to the horizon. A massive blanket of clouds was rolling towards us.

"Strange, the news didn't mention anything about rain," I said to myself. The clouds would probably just pass us by, even though the land desperately needed a shower.

I kept an eye out for John and Sophia. Both had errands to run in town, so I had given them lists of decorative items I needed.

To my surprise, the bath bombs with real rose petals that I had ordered from Mandy's Beauty Salon were ready today. Since my smartphone was still dead, I couldn't reach John or Sophia to let them know. So I had quickly set out myself to pick up the treasures for our bathrooms.

My stomach tingled with excitement because the bath bombs were - apart from the pending errands of my helpers - the last things that were missing, which meant our project would be finished by tonight at the latest. Really finished, as in everything-is-under-wraps-finished! I could hardly wait for the first guests to arrive. It would be in a week. The last time I was this excited was when I was almost eight years old and overheard that I would be getting a pony for my birthday.

Just before Sue's Diner, I slowed down a bit. There was a good chance that John and Sophia were there eating burgers and cake, because for the Keys, Sue's Diner was a must-visit when they were in Merryville. Nowhere did it taste as good as at Sue's; I had even missed her traditional cuisine in New York.

Though I couldn't see John or Sophia in the diner, I did see John's pickup truck in the parking lot behind it. My heart fluttered excitedly when I saw John standing behind his car, with his back to me. And then my heart stopped when I realized that Rachel was standing next to him. Very close to him, closer than I liked.

Their lips met, and my heart shattered into a thousand pieces.

I couldn't look away; it was like a horrible accident. In slow motion, I drove past the wreckage of my dreams that Rachel had brought crashing down with a single kiss. Again!

John and Rachel kissing in the middle of the public completely destroyed me.

John had already broken my heart once, which was bad enough, but a second time in the same way was crueler than I could bear.

The first question I asked myself was: Why? We had been happy, hadn't we?

And the second question that tormented me was: Why had he wanted to win me back in the first place?

Had I misjudged John, and was he a sadist who loved breaking hearts over and over again?

After another moment, I had lost sight of John and Rachel and steered my car with shaking hands towards the Interstate. I just wanted to get away from here, away from Merryville, away from the biggest mistake of my life that seemed to keep repeating itself.

Why don't we deserve a happy ending?

I fought against the tears that blurred my vision until I couldn't take it anymore and let them flow freely. My tears kept flowing, and I felt like they would never stop.

I should have gotten out, I thought. But then what? Pretend I hadn't seen anything?

Hello, what a beautiful day it is today!

Or should I have slapped John one after another? My fantasy of jumping in Rachel's face was also high on the list.

I tortured myself with what-if scenarios until I reached the Interstate, then even my sadistic thoughts had had enough of my tears. There was no point in thinking about missed opportunities because I couldn't change the situation anymore. But I could very well decide how to proceed. The decision I made now, whatever it was, would determine John's and my future.

I could run away by heading straight back to New York, or I could face the situation and get an answer to the question that was driving me almost insane.

Why did you break my heart again?

Head and heart engaged in a wild debate inside me.

I knew I was a master at running away because my flight instinct had haunted me all my life.

I could just do it again.

Running away hadn't worked last time, so I seriously considered trying a different strategy this time. What did I have to lose?

My - already broken - heart?

Defiantly, I wiped away the tears with my sleeve and turned my car around. I floored the gas pedal so I couldn't change my mind anymore and drove back to Merryville to confront John and Rachel.

My grief hid behind the anger that now protectively stood in front of the remains of my heart.

I could always flee to New York after John told me why he had trampled on our relationship.

Of course, John and Rachel were no longer there when I got back to Merryville.

Fate hated me; there was no other explanation for it. My karma score must have been deep in the negative, considering all the problems that plagued me.

Well, if John was no longer in Merryville, he must have driven back to *Red Rivers*. Then I'd just make a scene there, and he deserved at least a medium-sized scene!

I rushed to Red Rivers, leaving a huge cloud of dust behind me that almost reached the town. Except for Elli, who was standing in the round pen with Prime Tribute, no one was in sight. I took a deep breath, got out of the car, and had to control myself not to slam the door.

Then I stormed towards Elli. The poor thing had no idea what an idiot her brother was and why she was now bearing the brunt of his anger.

"Hey June," Elli greeted me with a smile, without taking her eyes off Prime Tribute. She let the black horse slow to a gentle trot.

"Where's John?" I asked. You could tell I had been crying; my voice was shaky and hoarse.

"What happened?" Elli asked. She lowered her crop, waited until Prime Tribute stood still, and then turned to me. When she saw my face, she left the round pen and hugged me.

"June? What's wrong?" she asked a second time.

The fact that John had fallen for Rachel a second time was playing on a loop before my eyes, but saying it out loud was harder than I thought.

"Is John alright?" Elli looked at me with concern.

"Yes," I answered dryly. John was doing great. Who knew what he and Rachel were up to right now, since he obviously wasn't here.

Because I didn't know how to start reporting what I had seen, I began at the beginning.

"I was in town, and I saw John there," I sobbed. Tears I could no longer hold back ran down my cheeks.

Elli looked at me, confused, and waited for me to go into more detail. There was no help for it; I had to get the truth out before it ate me up inside.

"I saw John with Rachel."

Elli's eyes widened. "What?!"

I nodded, sniffling, and Elli gave me a pitying look.

"This calls for a *Ben & Jerry's* crisis session. Give me a second. And after that, I need more details, okay?"

"Okay," I replied, wiping away my tears with my sleeve. "I'll wait by Champ."

"Got it, I'll be right back."

Elli ran to the main house to raid her huge ice cream stash, while I went to Champion's stall. My caramel-colored friend greeted me with a snort.

My God, I had almost driven away without saying goodbye to my best friend. I buried my face in his soft coat and tried to make up for my guilty conscience with extra petting.

"Champ, I swear to you, no matter where I go, I'll take you with me," I promised. Champ snorted loudly, which I interpreted as a clear *Yes*.

Elli entered the stall with two huge ice cream containers and looked at me questioningly.

"Strawberry Cheesecake or Cookie Dough?"

"Cookie Dough!" I answered decisively and took the ice cream container from her, which already had a spoon stuck in it.

"Oh wow, Houston. We have a really big problem," Elli said, and I had to grin briefly.

"You define problems by the choice of ice cream?"

"Who doesn't?" Elli asked, shrugging. "Strawberry Cheesecake is for medium problems, like a broken washing machine the night before a big party. Or a flat tire before a job interview. Cookie Dough, on the other hand, is the first choice for final boss problems."

"Final boss problems?" I laughed out loud and was grateful to Elli for managing to distract me.

"Yes. Now will you tell me exactly what happened?"

"Rachel happened," I said, without hiding my contempt for Rachel.

"Rachel is a really nasty final boss."

Elli calling her a final boss was really fitting. Since we'd known each other, she had been my biggest enemy, for whatever reason. No matter what I wanted, Rachel always ended up getting it in the end. Whether it was the last blouse in the shop, the limited and signed first edition of Bonnie Buckley's first album, or John.

"They kissed," I whispered, afraid that the echo of my voice would break my shattered heart even further.

"Shit." Elli immediately covered her mouth with her hands. It was the first time I had heard a female Key swear. "I know I should take it back. But in this situation, it was appropriate. And now I really need details."

"What do you want to know?" I asked bitterly. Just the thought that I would soon be the main topic of village gossip again created an uneasy feeling in the pit of my stomach. I didn't want to be the laughing stock of the people again or be pitied. I could really do without that.

"What kind of kiss was it?"

"Just a kiss."

"And how did they react when they saw you?"

"They didn't see me. I drove past them in the car."

"Just for the record, you saw everything but didn't do anything?"

I sighed. "Right."

I didn't mention that I had instead fallen into my old pattern and wanted to run away.

"I can't believe John did that willingly," Elli said seriously.

"I hardly think Rachel threatened him at gunpoint," I countered.

"He loves you, and only you. Everyone envies you for the looks he gives you."

"Then why did he do it?" I asked. New tears ran down my cheeks.

"There's definitely an explanation for that."

"I'm really curious about that one."

I thought about whether there was an explanation that could repair my broken heart, but I didn't have an answer to that.

"Hello?" Sophia's voice echoed through the stable. "Is anyone here?"

"We're in Champion's stall," Elli called back.

"June? Has John asked you yet?" Sophia asked, before she even saw us.

"Asked me what?"

"Never mind, not important! What are you doing here?"

When Sophia looked at our faces and our half-empty ice cream containers, she furrowed her brow.

"Is this a crisis meeting?"

"This isn't a crisis, this is an apocalyptic problem," I said, sniffling.

Elli leaned over the stall door. "June saw John and Rachel kissing in town earlier."

"What?" Sophia ran her hand through her blonde curls. "And you're sure?"

The sisters looked at me expectantly.

"If I wasn't sure, I wouldn't be standing here eating ice cream with you."

"Hm." Sophia took Ellis's ice cream bowl and thoughtfully spooned up the remaining ice cream. "There must be an explanation for this. First, John hates Rachel just as much as we do. Second, I was with him all morning and he kept raving about you. Third, John loves you, anyone can see that."

"Then why are they kissing in public?"

Sophia shook her head vigorously. "I have no idea. But it can't be the truth. You'll see, in the end, everything will be fine."

"How do you know that?" I asked. Usually, I liked to be infected by Sophia's enthusiasm, but I had burrowed myself into such a deep hole that even Sophia's radiant optimism couldn't reach me.

"June's right, sis. The evidence is overwhelming, and it's against John. The defense - us - urgently needs proof that he's innocent."

Sophia looked at us seriously. "The defense calls Sophia Key to the witness stand."

"Go ahead, Miss Key, tell the court what you saw," said Elli, mimicking a judge.

"I spent the morning with John, we went shopping together and then we were at Sue's to eat a piece of cake."

"One piece?" I asked, grinning. I just couldn't help myself. The fact that I had the strength for a joke made me believe that I could also find strength for everything else.

"Okay, okay. Four pieces of cake," Sophia admitted. "Anyway, John had planned to ask you if you wanted to work on the holiday ranch because we can't manage it alone."

Elli snorted softly. "A job offer is your defense? We knew from the start that we'd need someone to run the holiday ranch."

Sophia shook her head. "No. The job offer was just an excuse for him wanting you to stay, June."

John wanted me to stay? I felt a small part of my heart healing, but doubts remained, screaming loudly.

"Why didn't he want to ask me directly if I'd stay? Why through the job?" I asked.

Elli and Sophia both tilted their heads, then I found my answer myself.

"Because I didn't say anything last time."

Sighing, I rubbed my hands over my face. Why did I have to be so complicated? We might not even be facing this problem if I had simply said *yes* back then. But New York had caught up with me and suddenly I was afraid of change. The stupid thing was that inaction also led to things changing, I was feeling that now firsthand.

"We'll just wait for John and then we'll squeeze him like a lemon," said Elli, putting her hands on her hips.

"By any means necessary," her sister added.

I smiled at them gratefully and loved them for being on my side, even though John was their brother. They had actually managed to give me back my hope. My *happy ending* with John was far, far away, but it was no longer unreachable, and that meant we still had a chance.

We heard a car driving across the yard and my heart hammered wildly in my chest.

"How should I behave if it's John?" I asked.

"Show him honestly how you feel," Sophia advised me.

"And tell him to take off his hat when he talks to you," said Elli.

"Why should he take off his hat?" I asked, confused.

"Maybe he hit his head somewhere, then lost his memory and Rachel told him lies."

Not that I really wished John had a serious head injury, but that would be an explanation I could handle.

"Ready?" Sophia asked me with a smile.

No. But there were situations you were never ready for.

"Let's go," I said. Because I also knew that you only got rid of a fear by looking it directly in the eye.

"We've got your back," said Elli, patting me on the shoulder.

"Thanks."

I took a deep breath, wiped my damp cheeks dry, and tried to make my expression look as neutral as possible. I also prepared a few words that I wanted to throw at John right away. But once outside, they got stuck in my throat when I saw Rachel. Her usually perfectly styled blonde hair was tousled and her makeup was smeared. Her skin was slightly shiny and the white blouse she was wearing clung to her upper body. For me, there were only two scenarios that could have led to this image. Either she had been in the sauna fully dressed or... no! I forced myself not to finish my second thought.

"Elli, you should really hurry up with Prime Tribute, otherwise Rachel might move in here," Sophia whispered.

"I'm doing my best! But he's a really tough nut to crack," Elli replied.

"Girls, I need a plan B," I sighed.

"Smile nicely and wave!" Elli blurted out. "Don't let anything show, anything else would be grist to Rachel's mill."

"Okay," I said, even though I didn't know how I could even look Rachel in the eye. This beast had taken John away from me. For the second time!

"Hey, what's going on here?" Rachel asked when she saw us coming out of the barn with empty ice cream bowls.

"Girls' day with *Ben & Jerry's*," Sophia answered with a smile.

Elli and I nodded.

"Sounds good. I could use some ice cream right now," Rachel groaned, fanning herself with her hands. "It's insanely hot today."

"Yep, it's pretty muggy." Elli took a few deep breaths through her nose. "And it smells like a thunderstorm."

Elli was something like a flesh-and-blood weather station. If she announced a weather change, the weather would change.

How metaphorical that a storm was brewing right now, which had already announced itself this morning.

Rachel giggled. "Oh come on, not a single weather forecast predicted rain."

"Believe me, if your laundry is hanging outside, you should bring it in now," Elli replied.

"And we should move the horses away from the trees in the west paddocks," Sophia said seriously.

I nodded. "We should get to work right away." Then I looked at Rachel, who had been avoiding eye contact with me.

Did Rachel Pearson actually feel something like guilt? No, certainly not.

"If you're looking for John, he's in town," I said to Rachel as neutrally as possible. The sooner I got rid of her, the better.

"Oh, no. John and I were just engaged in a... let's say, heated discussion. I just wanted to check on Prime Tribute and see how he's doing."

Yeah, right, a *heated discussion* is what they had. Sophia, who had noticed my growing anger, put her hand on my shoulder and shook her head.

She's not worth it, her look said, but my anger claimed otherwise.

"Not much has changed since yesterday," Elli said bitterly. It frustrated her greatly that she couldn't help Prime Tribute.

"It'll be fine. See you, bye!" Rachel said goodbye, got into her car, and sped away.

"Okay, things don't necessarily look better now, but I'm sure there's an explanation for this too," Sophia sighed.

"So we're in agreement on how to interpret this *heated discussion*?"

Silence.

"Yeah, of course," I said bitterly. Even more bitter was the realization that there was nothing more to say. It couldn't be more obvious. John had cheated on me with Rachel, publicly and officially.

"You know what? I give up."

"June, don't say things like that," Sophia replied, horrified.

"Yes, Sophia's right. Don't take what Rachel said to heart," Elli added.

But I shook my head and let my tears flow freely. Even in the zero-point-period-zero-one percent chance that it wasn't what it looked like, Rachel would never stop until she could separate us again.

"I have to accept that there's no future for me here, no matter how much we all wished for it."

"And what do you want to do?" Elli asked cautiously.

"I'm going back to New York."

Both stared at me open-mouthed before protesting simultaneously. "No way!"

"If I go back to New York now, I might be able to save my company," I confessed to them what only John knew until now.

"You want to go back to a city where you can't find what you're looking for, to work in a job you hate?" Elli asked, frowning.

"Better than this painful back and forth," I answered, crying. How could I ever look John in the eyes again after he had hurt me so much? I was stuck in a vicious cycle, and the only way to break free was to leave Merryville.

"Yes," I said and stormed to my Mini. Elli and Sophia ran after me while I vented my anger to avoid feeling my broken heart.

"What was I thinking, getting involved with John a second time? I should have known better. No, I did know better, but I was stupid enough to listen to my feelings instead of my head."

Desperately, Elli and Sophia took turns trying to defend their brother, but their arguments simply bounced off me. Deep inside, I wished they would find an argument that would force me to pause, but they didn't.

"June, you can't drive in this state, especially not to New York!" Sophia appealed to my reason.

"Then I'll fly," I answered defiantly.

Elli and Sophia exchanged meaningful glances, then Sophia put her hand on my shoulder.

"I'm your friend. And if I can't convince you to stay, at least let me drive you to the airport before you cause a traffic accident."

Elli nodded. "I'd prefer to move the horses from the west paddock with you guys, but I can manage on my own."

"Thank you for understanding," I whispered.

Now Elli shook her head. "I don't understand you. But you're still family, and that's why I respect your decision, even if it's the dumbest decision you've ever made or will make."

I hugged Elli long and tightly.

"See you," I lied, because I didn't know if I would ever return to Merryville.

"You better!" Elli threatened me.

Then Sophia and I got into my car, and I took one last look at *Red Rivers*.

This time it was a farewell that would last forever; at least that's how it felt.

Chapter 20 – John

"Damn it!" I roared, shoving Rachel away from me. I was so enraged, I wanted to throw my pickup truck clear across the parking lot.

"But John," Rachel tried to explain, but my furious glare silenced her.

"You've already sabotaged my relationship with June once. I won't let it happen a second time. I only love June," I growled. My pulse was racing, pounding in my temples.

Rachel's dove-blue eyes filled with false tears. It wasn't her feelings I had hurt, but her pride. She was a Pearson, and a Pearson always got what she wanted. But Rachel couldn't have my heart because it didn't belong to me - it belonged to June.

"What were you thinking, Rachel?" I asked, shaking my head and looking around. No one was on the street; earlier, I had heard a single car pass by behind me. Good, at least no one had seen us. Gossip spread like wildfire in Merryville, and I couldn't deal with that right now.

"I don't know," Rachel answered, uncharacteristically meek.

"I'm going to ask June to move in with me today, and she'll say yes. Someday, I'll ask June to marry me, and she'll say yes to that too. June will be the only woman I ever ask these questions. Do you understand that?"

Rachel smoothed her white blouse and tried to avoid my gaze.

"John, I'm sorry," Rachel said. "How can I make it right?"

What? No hysterical fit? No slap? I scrutinized her facial expression closely because in no possible world was Rachel's humility genuine.

The longer I thought about her question, the angrier I became, because there was no excuse for what she wanted to do to June or for sabotaging our last relationship.

Damn it all!

Rachel trampled on decency and honor, so why was I the guy who felt bad about it? No idea how I was going to explain to June what had happened.

"John, say something!" Rachel commanded in a firm voice. There she was again, good old Rachel, who couldn't accept not getting what she wanted.

"You can make it right," I said. Rachel's eyes began to light up.

"Tell me how, and I'll do it!"

"First, you'll let Elli continue working with Prime Tribute, at double the price."

Rachel nodded.

"Second, you will never touch me again."

My gaze darkened, making it clear to Rachel what I thought of her. *Nothing.*

"Third, stay away from June and me."

Everything had been said now, and I vowed to never exchange another word with Rachel. Rachel stared at me, dumbfounded. You could see her thoughts racing in her gaze. Before she had time to answer me, I got into my car and drove out of town. I had to blow off some steam before I could return to *Red Rivers*.

Although I hadn't done anything wrong, I felt like an ass.

Until just now, everything had been so perfect. Our holiday ranch was almost finished, things between June and me had never been better, and I was sure she would be the mother of my children.

It drove me crazy that an insignificant kiss could destroy everything, but I couldn't let Rachel ruin our relationship a second time.

"Not this time," I growled aloud. By God, we were stronger than Rachel's desperate attempt to drive us apart.

It wasn't until I reached *Old Oaks*, a good forty miles from Merryville, that I turned back. Even though I still had no idea how to resolve the situation, I couldn't let time pass. It was never good to leave such things unspoken for too long. Was there a way to tell June the truth without hurting her?

Damn it, no. But I had to tell her; anything else would eat me up inside.

In a perfect world, June would understand everything, and we would continue to live happily as before.

In a world without consequences, I would have torched the Pearson estate out of anger.

But in the world we actually lived in, anything could happen, which felt frightening.

A loud thunderclap jolted me from my thoughts.

Well, that ends the calm before the storm.

The closer I got to *Red Rivers*, the bigger my worries grew, and when I turned into the driveway and saw our farm on the horizon, my worries were as big as the moon. I saw Elli on one of the paddocks. She was leading two horses at the same time while sitting on a third. The approaching thunder warned us of a storm that Elli had surely already smelled, otherwise most of the horses would still be in the west pasture. The trees there were good shade providers, but the falling branches during storms were too dangerous.

I slowed my truck. When Elli saw me, she let the two hand horses off the lead rope and galloped towards me. Her serious look didn't bode well; something must have happened. I got out of the car. Elli leaned on the horn of her western saddle.

"So, cooled off enough?" she asked, frowning.

What the hell? Could Elli suddenly predict more than just the weather?

"How do you know about that?" I countered.

"Rachel was here," Elli answered. She scrutinized me closely. I knew that look. Usually, Elli only looked at horses with huge aggression potential like that. With eagle eyes, Elli now paid attention to every micro-expression of mine, and I hid nothing.

"Rachel was here?" I clenched my fists in anger. Hadn't I made it clear enough to her that she should stay away from us? If Rachel had robbed me of the chance to explain myself...

"Yep. She told us about your heated conversation," Elli said, agitated.

Rachel had stuck to the truth and told them about our argument? My first thought was: Interesting, followed by my second thought: How could she still cause trouble despite the soul-baring?

"And what else did she say?"

I prayed to God for help and hoped that Rachel had kept the reason for our fight to herself.

Elli sighed, rubbing her forehead. "Isn't that enough?"

"Damn it, I don't understand anything! Stop speaking in riddles!" I snapped at her. The thought that Rachel had told her version of our kiss was driving me crazy. Then I took a deep breath to calm myself down. Elli didn't deserve my anger. A deep rumble of thunder announced the pitch-black clouds that were drawing ever closer to us.

"Unsaddle your horse, I'll take you in the truck," I said in a conciliatory tone.

"Good. And then we'll talk," Elli said, nodding. She dismounted and freed her horse from saddle and bridle, which she packed onto the bed of my truck.

"Why are you bringing the horses to the paddock alone? Where are June and Sophia?"

"That's exactly what we need to talk about," Elli sighed. "But first, you need to explain to me what's going on between you and Rachel."

The way Elli emphasized her words boded nothing good. Neither did the soft rumbling on the horizon.

"We should get to safety. Get in, I'll tell you everything in the truck."

The next clap of thunder shook me to my core. Elli jumped forward. It wouldn't be long before the storm broke over us.

We got into the truck and I tried to organize my thoughts.

"So, what's the deal with Rachel?" Elli pressed me seriously.

"There's nothing going on between Rachel and me, where did you get that idea?"

Elli bit her lip thoughtfully. "And what about the kiss?"

"Did Rachel claim that?" I probed.

"No," Elli answered. She was telling the truth, as I could always tell when my sister was lying.

"That was years ago," I waved it off. Before I told anyone else about it, it was a matter between June, me, and no one else.

"And the kiss today?" Elli's voice trembled.

I slammed on the brakes, kicking up sandy dust all around us.

"How do you know about that?"

"June saw you when she was driving through town. By the way, I'm fine, thanks for asking."

Fuck!

She was in the only vehicle that had passed us. No matter how you looked at it, June and I were under a bad star.

"Is she okay?" I asked. My voice sounded scratchy.

Elli snorted. "What do you think, idiot?"

"June didn't see me push Rachel away, did she?"

"Unfortunately not."

"Damn it." I looked at my little sister with a sigh. "Do you believe me?"

Elli studied me, then her serious expression softened a bit. "Of course. Sophia and I have always been on your side, even when the evidence was against you."

Relieved, I put the truck in first gear and drove on. If my sisters believed me, there was a chance June would too.

"I made it clear to Rachel once and for all that I love June."

"Rachel must have misunderstood something. To us, your heated conversation sounded like things were really heating up."

"Shit, no," I muttered. "I hope you didn't believe that crap."

Elli remained silent. Not a good sign.

If Rachel had managed to ruin my relationship, I swore to myself I'd make her life hell.

It wasn't until I parked the truck next to the main house that Elli broke her silence.

"We would never believe Rachel without proof, but I have to admit she sowed some doubt."

We got out of the truck and Elli hugged me to offer sisterly comfort. My pulse calmed a bit, and my hands were no longer shaking with anger, but I was far from feeling better.

"Where's June?" I asked. Elli tried in vain to suppress her sigh.

"June's gone, isn't she?" My voice sounded strange, raw and upset, just like the storm raging above us.

"She could have left right away, but she had decided to clear things up with you," Elli tried to defend June.

"And where is she now?"

Gone. Again. Of course June had run away, as she always did when things got serious.

"After Rachel's performance, it's no wonder she wanted to get away from here," Elli sighed.

I took a deep breath to suppress my rising anger, but I failed. To vent my frustration, I slammed my clenched fist against the driver's door of my truck, leaving a considerable dent.

"John!" Horrified, Elli grabbed my hand to check for injuries. My knuckles were red, but I barely felt the pain.

Why the hell did June always have to listen to her instincts? Did I mean so little to her?

"You should follow her, maybe you'll catch her before she gets on the plane," Elli said seriously.

She wasn't going by car, but flying? Even worse, because it showed that June wanted to disappear as quickly as possible.

Damn it, I was tired of constantly chasing after June. If I wasn't reason enough for her to stay at Red Rivers, then maybe - as painful as the realization was - it was better to just let June go.

"You shouldn't hold back travelers," I growled.

"You're just giving up?" Elli looked at me in disbelief. "That's not like you."

"People change. Or they don't," I answered bitterly.

"You two are made for each other, you love each other and you can't deny that."

"I won't chase after her like some faithful puppy," I repeated. I loved June with all my heart, but I was too tired, too disappointed to follow her.

If I wasn't worth staying for, June wasn't worth following—at least that's what I told myself.

"Okay, if you're determined to sabotage your relationship, fine. But then help me clean out the stalls before the storm hits. I don't want to be running across the yard with a wheelbarrow in the rain," Elli sighed.

"Whatever," I grumbled.

We went to the stable, where Prime Tribute was snorting and looking out from his stall.

Reflexively, I wanted to ask why he wasn't in the paddock with the other horses, then I remembered he was a hopeless case who didn't get along with his own kind.

I stroked his soft, black coat, then grabbed a pitchfork and tackled the first stall.

Even though Elli disagreed, I wondered if there were horses she couldn't help. She had been working with him for weeks without noticeable progress. It was time to face facts—there were situations and relationships that simply couldn't be saved.

The realization hit me hard.

June is gone.

No more bright green eyes to see myself reflected in, no more breath-stealing kisses. Damn it, I should have known from the start that June was just a visitor from the past.

"I'm such a damn idiot," I growled. Angrily, I flung the contents of my pitchfork into the wheelbarrow behind the open stall door.

"Yes, you are," Elli replied, mucking out the stall opposite.

One clap of thunder chased another, and the tension in the air crackled. It wouldn't be long before that tension broke.

"How could I ever believe June would stay here?"

"The more important question is: How can you let her go?"

"Shut up," I snapped at her, because Elli's way of appealing to my conscience was working better than I liked.

"But you're perfect together," Elli tried one last time.

"We never had a chance from the start. June runs away too easily, and I'm too proud to keep chasing after her."

Elli threw her pitchfork onto the wheelbarrow and came into my stall. She put her hands on her hips and took a deep breath as the next thunderclap cut through the silence like a sharp blade.

"Damn, nobody wants to be outside in this weather," I muttered.

"Yep," Elli answered, still ducking anxiously. "I hope the horses are okay."

I patted her upper arm. "You moved them all to the upper pastures, the horses are safer there than we are here in the stable."

"You're right. I'm just glad Prime Tribute is so calm."

I nodded. A panicked horse was hard to control, especially when you couldn't put it with the rest of the herd. Horses stayed much calmer in the herd during storms. It was all the more surprising that the black stallion was standing quietly in his stall, audibly chewing hay.

Elli leaned in conspiratorially.

"I don't want to jinx it, but I think Prime Tribute is up to something, he's so quiet," she whispered in a low voice. Then she cleared her throat and acted as if she hadn't said anything.

"You're the expert," I replied.

"What are you talking about?" she asked innocently. Then she grabbed her pitchfork and went to the last stall. "Just Nougat's stall left, then we're done."

I didn't know why, but I sensed what was about to happen. Elli snorted loudly and called out:

"Nougat's gone! Heaven help us, that goat needs a bell!"

I ran out of the stall to the other end of the stable where Elli was standing.

"I thought you'd made the stall escape-proof."

"So did I. We need to look for her," Elli sighed.

"I'm not letting you go outside in this storm," I growled.

Elli ignored me, went to the feed room, and got a bucket of mash that smelled like tea.

"Give this to Prime Tribute, it has herbs in it to keep him calm. Then we'll look for Nougat."

If June had ordered me around in that tone, I would have put her over my knee on the spot. But I couldn't refuse my little sister anything. Elli was the youngest Key, with the biggest eyes, and she shamelessly took advantage of it.

At least this way I didn't have to keep thinking about June. With each heartbeat, my pain grew.

I took the bucket, went to Prime Tribute's stall, and opened it.

"What the hell?"

I stood in front of the stall, dumbfounded, wondering if I had inhaled the herbs in the mash too deeply or if I could trust my eyes.

"You don't need to look for Nougat," I called to Elli.

"Nonsense, we're going out there, finding Nougat, and then I'm giving her a bell and a tracking device!"

"Get your bell ready. Nougat's in Prime Tribute's stall."

"What?" Elli let out a shrill scream and ran over to me. "Prime Tribute will kill Nougat!"

When Elli saw Prime Tribute and Nougat peacefully nibbling on the hay net side by side, she turned pale. Neither Elli nor I had ever seen the black stallion so relaxed with another animal.

"Wow. I really didn't expect that."

"Now you have your explanation for why he's been so calm this whole time," I said.

"How am I supposed to explain this to the Pearsons? Hello, we've solved the problem, he now has a goat buddy?" Elli asked me, frowning.

"I think when they see the end result, no explanation will be necessary."

Elli went into the stall and petted Prime Tribute and Nougat.

"Who would have thought that the loner and the runaway were made for each other?" Elli asked teasingly.

I raised an eyebrow and looked at her seriously.

Damn, she was right. If even these two hopeless cases - whom everyone else had given up on - could find each other despite their differences, weren't June and I meant to be together? My sisters certainly believed it, so why didn't June and I?

Prime Tribute was fiddling with Nougat's ear, while Elli examined me with a serious gaze.

"Back then, when you and June broke up for the first time and she left, what did you regret the most?"

"That I didn't follow her," I answered without thinking.

The pain of the past joined the current pain, and my temples began to throb painfully again.

Elli smiled at me. "Do you want June back?"

"Damn right, I do. But I shouldn't make the same mistake twice."

The realization hit me like a punch to the gut. I couldn't lose June a second time; the mere thought of it shredded my heart. And if I had to lasso her to make her stay, I would do it.

"What are you waiting for? If you're lucky, they're still at the holiday ranch. Sophia will buy you as much time as she can."

I took one last look at the odd duo and Elli. "Thanks for your help, sis."

I left the stable with quick strides.

"Don't you dare come back without June!" Elli called after me.

"That's not going to happen," I answered determinedly.

June belonged to me.

I wouldn't allow June to run off with my heart again. No way. Her place was by my side, and no matter how fast or far she ran, this was her home, this was where her heart belonged. And I knew exactly how I would convince her of that.

Chapter 21 – June

I loaded my halfheartedly packed suitcase into Sophia's car. Hopefully, I scanned the horizon for John, but saw nothing except pitch-black clouds drawing ever closer. There were thousands of reasons why I had to leave, but if John had given me just one reason to stay, I would have. But he wasn't here. John's failure to show up finally broke my heart.

Sophia had been trying alternately to comfort me or to stop me from packing my things and leaving. But no one, except John himself, could stop me now. I had booked a one-way ticket for late afternoon. Deep down, I had hoped to catch a flight back for tomorrow, giving John more time to stop me, but on the other hand, I wanted to get away from here as quickly as possible. I was afraid that John and Rachel...

I slammed the trunk shut to interrupt my train of thought.

"Finished packing?" Sophia asked.

"Yes, I'm almost done. But one thing is still missing." I bent down to take off Sophia's boots that I had been wearing the whole time.

Sophia waved it off. "No, please keep the boots."

"But you love your boots, all of them," I replied.

"I insist that you take at least a small piece of home with you to New York."

I gratefully took Sophia in my arms. As I did so, I let my gaze wander over the pitch-black sky. The weather was a mirror of my soul, gray and turbulent.

"We should get going, the storm could start any moment," I whispered.

"Okay." Sophia took the keys from me and we got into the car. My heart told me to hold on to the holiday ranch, my true, only home I ever had, but my mind forced me not to look back.

"What are we going to do with your Mini?" Sophia asked after we had left Merryville behind.

"You can keep it," I sighed. "In the big city, there are plenty of ways to get to your destination."

"You can't just give me your car," Sophia replied, stunned.

"Why not? You gave me your boots," I said, clicking my heels together.

"That's completely different," Sophia snorted.

"What do you suggest I do with the Mini?" I asked conciliatorily.

Sophia looked at me with bright eyes. "I'll drive it to New York for you when I get the chance, and then you can show me the city, okay?"

"Okay."

Then it got quiet between us. Only the increasingly loud thunder cut through the oppressive silence.

"Are you really sure?" Sophia sighed softly.

"That you can visit me?" I played dumb and hoped Sophia would leave it at that.

"June, you know exactly what I mean. Do you really want to go back to New York?"

No.

"I have to," I answered and took a deep breath.

"John is an idiot, but he loves you. He surely doesn't want you to leave."

Tears blurred my vision. "If he really wanted that, he would have come."

"We can still wait," Sophia said hopefully, but I shook my head.

"No, I've waited long enough for John to follow me."

"And Champ? Do you want to leave him behind again?"

"We'll figure out how to get him to New York somehow," I answered. I had no idea how I could get my horse from Texas to New York, but somehow it had to be possible.

I hated Sophia for asking me so many questions I had no answer to. It thundered and we both flinched. I pondered whether this thunderclap was a warning or a confirmation.

If I left Merryville now, it would be forever.

I had the choice between a safe but unhappy life in New York or a happy life at Red Rivers that could cost me my heart.

My mind had had enough of here, enough of romantic promises that were broken, enough of John's hazel eyes that surveyed me possessively, enough of his touches that still tingled even now.

Stop lying to yourself, June!

My heart was broken, yes, but it recognized the lies immediately. I hadn't had enough of John, but I had had enough of Rachel.

It was good that this storm had broken out right now, because Sophia had been close to convincing me to turn back. Deep inside, I still hadn't given up hope that everything was a silly misunderstanding.

When we had left Merryville behind, I could finally breathe again. Whether it was due to the heavy rain or because I was bringing my heart to safety, I didn't know.

"Tell me about New York!" Sophia broke the silence.

I swallowed the thick lump stuck in my throat.

"You want to know more?" I asked. Of course, I had answered hundreds of Sophia's questions - multiple times - but she couldn't get enough of New York.

Whatever. As long as Sophia wanted to know more about New York, she wasn't torturing me about John.

"I want to know everything," she answered with a smile. "Where does the coffee taste best?"

In our holiday cabin, when John brings it to me in bed, wearing only jeans.

"The coffee tastes the same everywhere in New York," I replied.

"And where's the most beautiful sunrise?"

On horseback, at the highest point of Red Rivers.

"Actually, only outside the city," I said gloomily. No matter what question Sophia asked, the first things that popped into my head were memories, images, and moments far from New York.

Sophia peppered me with more questions.

"When does the first snow fall in New York?"

Just the thought of the biting cold air that prevailed in New York all winter long gave me rheumatic pains in my knee joints.

"By December at the latest, New York will be buried under a blanket of snow."

"I imagine it must be dreamy to walk across a snow-covered Times Square," Sophia gushed. "It must be romantic to kiss in front of the

Christmas tree at Rockefeller Center or take a carriage ride through Central Park."

For the rest of the drive, Sophia told me about her visions of New York, how she would stumble into the arms of her dream man and assert herself in the big city against all odds.

I wondered if Sophia's unshakeable optimism could be an asset to New York, or if she wouldn't be better off in *Red Rivers*. It was her home, with everything that came with it. Wait, was I talking about Sophia or myself?

We left the heavy storm behind us, only the rain followed us to Brownsville.

When we reached the airport, Sophia parked my Mini near the entrance.

Swallowing hard, I entered the main hall, closely followed by Sophia, who gaped at the display boards with flight numbers.

"Wow, so many flights to all over the world!"

I grinned briefly, as the airport in Brownsville could easily fit two dozen times into JFK Airport in New York. There was one international flight to Mexico City and one to Montreal; all other flights led to New York or cities on the West Coast.

"Wait until you see JFK Airport, where passengers are transported by *AirTrain* because the grounds are so vast."

"You take a train to your plane?" Sophia asked. Her eyes grew huge, then she started laughing and ran her hand through her blonde curls. "Heavens, I'm such a country bumpkin!"

I smiled at her. "I've always enjoyed being a country bumpkin. There's nothing wrong with that."

Sophia tilted her head and looked at me thoughtfully.

"Then why aren't you one anymore?"

I remained silent, because we both knew the answer to that.

The lump in my throat grew thicker as I heard a flight being called over the loudspeaker system. I looked at my watch. It wouldn't be long before my flight was called. My heart grew heavier as the farewell drew nearer.

Why hadn't John stopped me? One look would have been enough to make me stay.

Making a decision had been painful, but necessary.

Sighing, I looked around the manageable hall until my gaze settled on the empty counter.

"I should get my ticket." The words felt as heavy as lead.

"I'll go with you as far as I'm allowed," Sophia said, smiling. She held out her arm and I linked mine with hers. Her emotional support did me good, and in no time I was holding my printed ticket in my hand.

The flight ticket felt as heavy as a ton, and I had the feeling I couldn't breathe again.

Breathe. Life goes on, June!

But that was exactly what scared me! The world just kept turning as if nothing had happened, when everything had changed!

Our next stop led us to the security area at the other end of the hall. My small suitcase counted as hand luggage; I had only brought the essentials. I had said goodbye to most things because they smelled of John or evoked a memory of him.

We stopped in front of the security checkpoint.

"I guess this is it then," Sophia said sadly. She bit her lower lip to hold back her tears.

"Please don't cry, or I'll have to cry too," I pleaded, sobbing.

Sophia hugged me. "I'll miss you, we all will!"

"I'll miss you all too," I replied.

As we separated, Sophia started giggling. "Grams had even brought out our old toys from the basement because everything was screaming for offspring."

"Your grandma really doesn't waste any time," I said, grinning.

Sophia shrugged and blew a blonde curl out of her face.

"Well, we have to make up for the lack of women somehow."

I patted Sophia on the shoulder. "You have a wonderful family."

"Yes. And you're still part of it."

With each passing second, it became harder for me to leave, because Sophia was reminding me of everything I was leaving behind - namely, everything.

The next loudspeaker announcement made me flinch; it was a call for my flight.

I had never been good at saying goodbye, but I had to get through this now.

"I'll see you soon in New York," I said with a shaky voice.

"Okay." Sophia smiled bravely at me. "If you change your mind, you'll find me at *Burger2Go*."

Sophia and I hugged one last time, silent and tearful, then our paths diverged. She retreated, and I sniffled my way through security. The security staff paid me no special attention; minor to moderate dramas were everyday occurrences at any airport.

After clearing security, my gaze fell on my phone. I hadn't tried to turn it on for days.

Should I give it a try?

My unbridled curiosity finally convinced me to at least attempt it.

At first, the display only lit up briefly, then went dark again, and finally started up normally as if it had never been broken.

Was this a sign that my old life in New York was continuing?

A rainbow shimmered around the deep cracks of the touchpad, but I could see that I had dozens of missed calls, which made my heart beat faster.

Was it John, trying to stop me from making the biggest mistake of my life? I was ready to let him stop me!

The butterflies in my stomach, thought to be dead, fluttered again. Unfortunately, only until I saw that the calls were from Frank. One by one, the butterflies disappeared.

Good Lord, what am I doing here?

Over the loudspeakers came the announcement that my flight was ready for check-in, and the first people streamed towards the open jetway.

I stood up and stared through the window at the large plane that was supposed to take me to New York.

My legs carried me towards the plane, but my heart fought against it, wanting to return to Merryville.

To organize my thoughts and calm my pounding heart, I stopped briefly and took a deep breath. As if in time-lapse, more and more passengers rushed to the entrance of our aircraft, and one call followed another.

Admittedly, it felt wrong to leave, but I had come so far that it seemed impossible to turn back.

Just one look would have been enough, John...

My flight was called for the last time, and I made a final decision.

All this time, my head and heart had been fighting each other, but that was over now. Sometimes in life, you stand at a turning point that forces you to make decisions. I didn't like that I was standing at such a turning point, but I couldn't change it. I was forced to decide, and when I realized how final the decision was, the answer came to me quite simply.

I unlocked my broken phone and dialed Frank's number as I took the heaviest steps of my life.

From today, my escape is over. For good.

Chapter 22 – John

THE DAMN RAIN JUST wouldn't stop. It was pouring buckets and thundering every second. I had missed June at the holiday ranch, God knows how far she was from me now. But it didn't stop me from following her. And if I had to drive all the way to New York, I'd do it for June!

You can run all you want, baby. I'll follow you.

Once June was back here, she wouldn't get away from me so easily. My favorite rope, the gag, and my hand were waiting for a good, classic spanking - which June more than deserved.

How could she leave me standing in the rain? Well, how could I let her go?

Everything had changed, but we were still the same as before.

As fast as the storm allowed, I drove to Brownsville. I soon left the storm behind, but the rain had stuck to my heels and was a persistent follower.

Arriving at the airport, my heart leaped when I saw June's Mini parked just before the entrance. So there was a chance June was still here, otherwise Sophia would have driven back long ago.

I desperately searched for an empty parking spot, and the further I moved away from the airport entrance again, the tenser I became. Absurd! June's flight could take off any second, and only a few meters separated us from our *happy ending*.

To make matters worse, a large tour bus blocked the road for half an eternity to let its passengers disembark.

Angrily, I hit the steering wheel, not wanting to admit that a missing parking spot was our downfall.

Finally, the bus started moving again. Agonizingly slowly, I moved further and further away from the airport, with no prospect of a free parking spot.

A plane rolled onto the runway, accelerated, and took off. What if that was June's flight? At the beginning of the runway, the next plane was already waiting. The planes were taking off every minute, and the deep roar of the turbines sent a shiver down my spine.

"Shit, no!" I cursed loudly, slammed on the brakes, and parked the car in the second row. I didn't care if it got towed, I couldn't wait any longer. I got out of the car and ran as fast as I could to the airport entrance. The wind whipped the rain into my face, my cowboy hat could only protect me from a small part of it.

The cold drops burned on my skin but couldn't diminish my determination. My lungs burned, just like my calves, as I ran back across the sprawling grounds. I felt like I was in a damn nightmare, because the longer I ran, the longer the distance seemed to become.

Fuck, fuck, fuck!

Why was I such an idiot? I should have pushed Rachel away much earlier, just as I should have held onto June much tighter, back then.

No woman had ever gotten under my skin like June. Even when she had long been gone, I only had feelings for her, all other women had been uninteresting.

Breathing heavily, I finally reached the damn entrance and looked around. The tour group that had blocked me earlier was now blocking my view again.

My restless gaze scanned the surroundings for June's brown hair and emerald eyes. In vain.

The airport wasn't big, yet I had lost my bearings. My racing heart was beating so loudly that it drowned out even the loud conversations and announcements echoing through the entrance area.

I pushed my way recklessly through the group to get a better view of the departure boards. The only flight to New York shown there was scheduled to depart in two minutes. Through the large glass window, I could even see the plane. A large machine that was just detaching the jetway.

Damn it!

I ran to the nearest counter, startling the employee behind it.

"I need to get on the flight to New York!" I barked at her.

The young employee looked first at me, then at the plane I was pointing to.

"I'm sorry, sir, but if you didn't respond to the final call, there's nothing I can do for you."

"I just got here, but I absolutely have to get on that plane!"

She smiled at me with professional friendliness, but beneath her neutral, completely made-up expression, I could see that her finger was already on the security button that would call for backup.

So I took a deep breath to continue speaking in a calmer tone.

"The love of my life is on that plane, and I need to stop her from making the biggest mistake of her life."

The young blonde looked at me in surprise; she probably hadn't expected this explanation. She squinted her eyes and looked me up and down, then gave me a pitying look.

"That's really romantic, but I can't do anything for you. I don't have the authority, but I could offer you a later flight to New York."

"When?" I asked. The employee's fingers flew swiftly over the keyboard, then she turned her screen so I could see it.

"Tonight," she said with a practiced smile. "There are still seats available in first and business class. Shall I make a reservation for you?"

Impulsively, I wanted to book the flight, but then what? June's phone was broken, I didn't know where she lived or where her office was, if it even still existed. It would be idiotic to hope to randomly run into June in a city of millions like New York.

"No, that's not going to help," I sighed.

"Then I'm afraid there's nothing I can do for you, sir."

"I guess not," I muttered. As if hypnotized, I watched June's plane as it now rolled onto the runway. Even if I somehow made it through security, I couldn't reach the plane anymore.

"Sir? Would you please clear the counter?" the blonde pulled me out of my thoughts.

A small line had formed behind me, just like at the counters to my left and right.

I nodded politely to the employee and the other people waiting and left the counter to return to the display board. My temples were throbbing painfully and my muscles were so tense that I could have smashed through granite with them.

Someone put their hand on my shoulder from behind.

"John?"

I turned around and looked directly into my sister's eyes.

"She's gone," I sighed.

"Yes, she's gone," she said thoughtfully. In her hand, she held a half-eaten burger with extra bacon. Just the sight of it made me feel sick, and the smell intensified my nausea.

"How can you think about food right now?" I asked her reproachfully. For a brief moment, I had forgotten that my sisters could eat in all life situations. Good mood eating, bad mood eating, Ben & Jerry's emergency eating, they found a reason for everything and nothing.

"Just so you know, I'm not enjoying it," Sophia snorted.

I frowned. The situation was more serious than I thought. Sophia had never not enjoyed a burger, especially not one with extra bacon.

"I'm sorry, it's not your fault. I should have been faster."

Sophia hugged me. "It's okay. You're here and you tried to stop her. That's all that matters."

The plane to New York roared its turbines, accelerated, becoming smaller and smaller until it was just a tiny dot on the horizon.

There she flew away, the love of my life.

June was gone, but her scent remained. More than that, it was getting stronger, and I hated my mind for torturing me with old memories.

"No. I failed, and that's what will remain in the end. John, who was always too proud to catch his fleeing June. *And they both lived lonely ever after.*"

"What a terrible ending." June's voice echoed in my head. Had I finally lost my mind?

Sophia looked behind me and started beaming, then cleared her throat. "I think my burger tastes good again. And over there," she pointed to a seating area right in front of the panoramic window, "it probably tastes even better."

What the hell?

I turned around and looked into tear-filled emerald eyes.

"June?"

Could I trust my eyes? Yes. June Farley, the love of my life, was truly standing in front of me.

"What are you doing here?" I asked, dumbfounded. It didn't matter! All that mattered was that I had the chance to say what I needed to say! "I'm sorry I'm late."

"You're here," June whispered. Her voice now sounded weak and fragile.

"And so are you," I replied.

The tension between us was palpable, and the unspoken words screamed deafeningly loud.

"I'm sorry you had to see Rachel kiss me. But I pushed her away and made it clear that I only love you. You're the woman I want to have children with and grow old with."

June looked at me with wide eyes. "I know."

"What can I do to make it right?" I asked.

"You don't have to do anything, John."

"What..."

Slowly, June placed an index finger on my lips to silence me. Her touch was proof that she was really standing in front of me. She wasn't a ghost, not a hallucination, not a mirage.

Still, my muscles tensed again because I didn't know what her words meant.

June took a deep breath while keeping her eyes on me. "I should have known you weren't having an affair with Rachel, but seeing you two together hurt so much that I couldn't help but run away."

I growled softly. June's heart was broken, and it was my fault. She had fled from me - rightfully so. But, and this was the most important thing, she was standing in front of me at this moment.

"John?" June asked me quietly. "Can you forgive me for running away without hearing your side of the story?"

"Damn, June," I muttered and looked at the next plane making its way to the runway. "You ran away, yes, but you didn't follow through with your escape. Instead, you chose to stay here. Just like I chose - almost too late - to follow you."

I had been wrong, June and I weren't the same as before, we had changed. We had grown up, become more mature and wise enough to hold onto each other.

Otherwise, June would be on her way to New York now, and I'd be on my way to Sue's Diner to get drunk.

June sniffled softly. "I just couldn't get on the plane, I couldn't do it, I love you too much for that."

Smiling, I wiped a tear from her face. "I'm damn glad about that, I love you too, June."

The tension in the air that had separated us disappeared, and we fell into each other's arms. Our lips met, and sparks flew. Her honey-sweet, soft lips on mine were proof that everything was alright again.

"I'm never letting you go again, damn it," I growled.

"I hope so," June replied. "But how do you plan to do that?"

Grinning and challenging, I looked at June. Normally, I gave June such looks just before I put her over my knee, which is why her cheeks reddened. But this time, it wasn't June who went down on her knees, but me. There was no question in my mind that June would be the mother of my children, and I hoped June saw it the same way.

She looked at me with wide eyes, and Sophia, who had just been at the other end of the hall, appeared behind June.

"I could just catch you with the lasso again, but that might seem strange to others under certain circumstances. So there's only one other way I can tie you to me. We belong together, and I want everyone to know that. June Farley, will you be my wife?"

My words felt right because they came directly from my heart. Hopefully, they were enough to heal June's broken heart.

Her sniffling turned into loud sobbing, and she tormented me for what felt like an eternity until she nodded. "Yes, I will be your wife!"

I jumped up, lifted June by her hips, and spun her around in joy. My spontaneous marriage proposal was met with applause from some of the passengers, but at that moment, I only had eyes for June, whose bitter tears had transformed into tears of joy.

When I set her down again, we kissed once more, hungrily. I simply couldn't get enough of her and her sweet lips. Our tongues intertwined, and the mixture of adrenaline, joy, and relief quickly led me to indecent thoughts.

Restraint. You have your whole damn life to love June in every way imaginable.

Sophia hugged June, and they both squealed excitedly.

"Congratulations! It's about time you two found each other," Sophia said, smiling.

June returned her smile, then stared at her boots. "I'm still keeping the shoes though."

"Okey-dokey, consider it an early wedding gift."

They hugged each other a second time, then Sophia embraced me.

"Well done, bro. I'm proud of you!"

I looked at Sophia with a serious expression that said *thank you for everything*. She and Elli had talked some sense into June, and I was certain that without my two sisters, the whole situation would have turned out quite differently.

"So what now?" Sophia asked.

"We go home and celebrate," I answered.

June linked her arm with mine. "Definitely. Your grandma is going to flip out."

"And Elli even more so," I added, grinning. "Speaking of Elli, she's cured Prime Tribute's loneliness in a flash. He's finally found a girlfriend."

"What?" Sophia asked, astonished.

June also looked at me in surprise. "How did she manage that so quickly?"

"With Nougat," I answered briefly. That left them both speechless.

Yeah, who would have thought that Rachel's elite show jumper would befriend a goat? Admittedly, it was just as likely as the possibility of June and me finding our *happy ending*. But there we stood, happy and in love, amused by Prime Tribute and Nougat.

"Well, anyway, it's a shame about the wasted flight to New York," Sophia sighed.

June's eyes lit up briefly, then she pulled her plane ticket out of her pocket and handed it to Sophia.

"Just because I didn't find my happiness in New York doesn't mean yours isn't there. We can probably have the flight transferred to you. You can stay in my apartment and check out New York."

Sophia held her breath in excitement. "Really?"

"Really!" June replied.

My sister, alone in the big city? The thought made me a bit uneasy for a moment, but Sophia had been raving about New York since she was a little girl. Sometimes I also forgot how quick-witted Sophia actually was. If anyone could stand up to the New York office big shots, it was Sophia, no question.

"But you'll be back for the wedding at the latest," I said in a half-serious tone.

"Absolutely! And when is it happening?"

June and I looked at each other. "As soon as possible," we said simultaneously.

"That's enough time to explore the city," Sophia said, beaming. "What are the chances of a spontaneous blizzard with lots of snow in the summer?"

"With all the miracles happening lately? Not bad," I said with a wink and put my arm around the greatest miracle that had ever happened to me.

Epilogue – June

"I can't breathe anymore," I gasped, clinging to Sophia, who looked at me with concern. Elli, standing behind me, loosened the corset laces. Despondently, I sank onto my bed. I wanted nothing more than to hide under the covers and wait for the day to be over.

"Take deep breaths, June. You can do this," Sophia tried to encourage me while nodding to Elli.

I wasn't exactly having cold feet, but it would be a lie to say I was feeling good. I was far from feeling fine!

Heavens, my hormones were running wild. Not to mention that Elli and Sophia were even more excited than I was, which made me even more nervous.

"We have to face it, my dress has become too tight," I managed to say.

"Ditto," Elli replied, strained. For a solid twenty minutes, the three of us had been trying to squeeze me into my wedding dress.

"But the dress fits you like a glove," Sophia sighed.

"It did," I snorted, and Sophia rubbed her tired eyes. She had only returned from New York the day before yesterday and had spent all of yesterday planning the wedding at *Red Rivers*. I had entrusted all the planning to my two bridesmaids while John and I had been taking care of the holiday ranch.

Oh John, I miss you!

We hadn't seen each other since last night. He had been out with his brothers and two barrels of beer, while Elli, Sophia, and I had watched the entire first season of *Sex and the City* in sweatpants with a ton of sweets.

We were all three so excited that we hadn't gotten a wink of sleep.

Good grief, why hadn't I tried on the dress last night for a test run? Then we would have had all night to find a solution. But now? There were only a few hours left until the wedding, and I had no dress!

Oh God!

"Yes, it did," I said, breathing heavily and looking at myself in the mirror. I was wearing my grandma's wedding dress, and I looked damn enchanting in it because it was perfect... only *we* didn't quite fit into it anymore.

"I can't imagine that our *Ben & Jerry's gossip sessions* had anything to do with it, but there's a slight chance they might have," Elli said innocently, which made me laugh.

"No, the daily bowl of ice cream surely has nothing to do with it," I giggled. My laughter disappeared as quickly as it had come and was replaced by tears. "I can't walk down the aisle without a dress."

"Please don't cry, June, we'll figure this out," Sophia tried to comfort me. But once the tears had fought their way up, there was no holding them back.

It had been like this for weeks, and there was no improvement in sight. How did John even put up with me? I could barely stand myself, being as emotional as I was.

"What should I do?" I asked desperately. There was no chance the dress would close.

Elli stood next to Sophia. "You could wear a potato sack, and John would still find you beautiful."

I didn't know whether to laugh or cry at this statement, so I just looked at Elli in confusion.

"Okay, I have an idea," Sophia said, thoughtfully running her fingers through her blonde curls. "I'll get Grams, she has a solution for everything."

"That's good! We'll wait here and take care of the makeup," Elli added.

I nodded, grateful that the two sisters seemed more composed than the situation actually warranted - it calmed me immensely. Through the window, I watched Sophia leave the holiday ranch in the car.

I sighed heavily. "I hope they hurry."

"We'll find a solution, I promise," Elli said. Then she took care of my hair, which had large curlers in it.

As if Elli had never done anything else, she styled my hair.

Sooner than expected, Sophia returned with her grandma in tow. Mary was still wearing a cooking apron; Sophia must have kidnapped her from the kitchen. Both were loaded down, Sophia with a large garment bag, Mary with a sewing machine.

"What's the situation?" Mary asked.

"Catastrophic!" I answered. "I don't fit into the dress, and I have no idea where we're going to get a new one at such short notice."

"Lucky you, sweetheart. I know exactly where we're going to get a new dress." Smiling, Mary set her sewing machine on the table. She pointed at my dress with her index finger. "Take it off, now!"

I blushed, but I seized every chance to become a perfect bride. Then Sophia opened the garment bag and unpacked another wedding dress. It was simpler than my dress, but timelessly beautiful.

"This is Grandma's wedding dress," Sophia explained.

"And what do you plan to do with it?" I asked critically.

"We're going to merge the two dresses and make a traditional Farley-Key dress out of them," Mary said.

Sophia fiddled with the hem of the dress. "You were so excited about keeping it traditional and connected to home that we thought this was a good idea."

I felt tears fighting their way up again, but I bravely held them back so my eyeliner wouldn't smudge.

Sophia looked at me with concern. "Don't you like the idea?" She looked painfully at the group of women. "Oh no, she doesn't like the idea! Do we have a Plan C?"

Elli placed a reassuring hand on Sophia's shoulder, then looked at me.

"June, it's your day, we'll do whatever you tell us to do."

"Should I pack the dress away again so it doesn't make you cry anymore?" Sophia asked me cautiously.

"No. I'm not crying because of the dress." I shook my head. "Well, I am crying because of the dress, but only because I think the idea is perfect."

Mary clapped her hands joyfully. "Well then, let's get to work, girls. We have a lot to do, and the dress shouldn't look like it was thrown together at the last minute."

As I put on one of John's loose shirts, I watched as Sophia, Elli, and Mary descended on my wedding dress together.

Sophia kept glancing at me. Understandable. I was a hormone-plagued, emotional bride who was about to walk down the aisle but had no wedding dress. Who wouldn't worry that the bride might lose it?

"I promised you the perfect wedding and you're going to get it," Sophia assured me for the second time. She smoothed out a large piece of fabric that Mary was working on with the sewing machine.

"Thank you all for believing in this." I smiled at everyone. My only wish was for the wedding to become the main topic of conversation in Merryville, so that news would reach the Pearson estate that I would be *Mrs. John Key* by noon.

My heart fluttered with excitement at the thought that John and I would really be getting married today.

Elli, who was busy measuring and cutting the other dress, hummed Bonnie Buckley's greatest hit, and I watched as the *Farley-Key hybrid dress* slowly took shape. Every adjustment, every cut, and every instruction seemed perfect, at least from the outside. I could finally start to relax a bit, seeing how methodically the three of them were working.

"This isn't your first project together, is it?" I asked.

Sophia shook her head. "No. We used to sew together all the time."

"We should do it more often," Elli agreed.

"When was the last time either of you wore something I sewed for you, hm?" Mary asked dryly, and they both joined in her laughter.

"Okay, okay. No dresses or blouses for us. But we could use new saddle pads and horse blankets," Elli said thoughtfully.

"And I need lots of scarves for New York. It's pretty cold there in the winter, and I really want to walk through Central Park when it's snowy," Sophia added.

Ever since she'd returned from her New York trip, Sophia had been raving about nothing but the ice-cold New York winter.

"So you really want to move to New York?" I asked.

"Not if Mom has anything to say about it," Sophia sighed briefly. "But by the time it happens, I'll have worn her down."

"We'll see, sis," Elli said with a grin.

"As long as you promise not to forget our Christmas traditions, I'll keep your mother off your back," Mary said so dryly that we all had to laugh.

Sophia put her hands on her hips indignantly. "I would never miss our Christmas celebration!"

The Keys' Christmas celebration was legendary, as on Christmas Eve, Keys from all over the world gathered at *Red Rivers* to celebrate together. Sue's Diner had its highest-grossing month of the entire year in December, thanks to the Keys alone.

Then Sophia cleared her throat and continued in a low voice. "The only way I'd miss it is if my dream man asked me to have a white Christmas with him."

Mary waved it off. "Who needs snow when you've got my homemade eggnog?"

"Oh yes, the eggnog spectacle is amusing every year," Elli giggled. No one joined in because no one knew what she meant. "Oh, never mind. It's an inside joke and it should stay that way."

Judging by Elli's face, the inside joke was pretty funny, because she was still grinning. I was in good company, but I just couldn't laugh along, the situation was far too serious for that.

My apartment looked like a battlefield, with scraps of fabric, threads, and scissors strewn everywhere. Not to mention that I was supposed to walk down the aisle shortly and my wedding dress was lying half-cut on the table. They kept wrapping measuring tapes around my upper arms, hips, or thighs.

I started sobbing again. "I'm sorry, I don't know what's wrong with me."

Sophia, who was just working on the hem of the hybrid dress, looked up. "It's your wedding day, of course you're emotional."

"Exactly. Every bride goes through this," Elli backed up her sister.

Mary, on the other hand, looked at me with a motherly-stern gaze. "You know exactly what's going on, sweetie."

I flinched because I hadn't told anyone about my condition yet. I definitely didn't want to announce that John and I were expecting a child before our wedding. We lived in Texas, and I didn't want anyone to think John was marrying me just because of my pregnancy.

"I don't know what you mean, Mary," I said innocently.

"Of course you don't." Mary winked at me.

How did Mary even know about it? I didn't have a baby bump yet, I had hidden the pregnancy test in a burglar-proof spot, and John didn't even know about our happiness yet because I wanted to wait for the perfect moment to tell him.

"Wait a minute!" Sophia's confused gaze shifted between Mary and me. "What's going on between you two?"

Damn! Mary had let the cat out of the bag, and there was definitely no putting that kitten back in. Elli and Sophia were eyeing me with equal hunger for sensation.

"We need to search for clues, sis. They're hiding something from us," Elli chimed in.

"Right. Clue number one: mood swings," Sophia began.

"I'm a bride without a wedding dress, of course I'm going crazy!" I tried to save myself.

"Which brings us to clue number two: You don't fit into your wedding dress anymore," Elli added.

"And that's because of our daily Ben & Jerry's consumption, which you got me hooked on, Elli!" I felt cornered but didn't want to throw in the towel yet.

"And with that, you lead us directly to the third and final clue: Peppermint ice cream!"

"What's wrong with peppermint?"

Elli tossed her blonde curls back. "No one has ever brought peppermint ice cream into our house. Peppermint ice cream tastes like mouthwash!"

As Elli got so worked up about the peppermint topic, I had to laugh.

"Yeah, I thought so too until recently, until I tried it. It's delicious!" I replied, giggling.

Elli and Sophia looked at each other in shock.

"June is pregnant," they both blurted out simultaneously, and I threw Grandma Key a pained look. "Thanks, Mary."

"Well, the cat's out of the bag now," she said with a half-apologetic look.

Immediately, Elli and Sophia dropped their work to hug me, squealing.

"Congratulations! Is it a boy or a girl?" Elli burst out.

I rubbed my belly where our little bundle of joy was growing. "The doc couldn't tell for sure yet, but it feels to me like it's a little cowgirl."

"How exciting! We're going to be aunts and get some female support! I'll teach the little one everything she needs to know to hold her own against the horde of men here," Elli gushed.

Sophia, who was a bit more reserved, asked, "John doesn't know about this, does he?"

I shook my head. "No. I wanted to tell him after the wedding." Then I cast a serious look around the room. "That's why this conversation can never go public."

"You got that, girls? You're really not good when it comes to secrets," Mary backed me up.

Sophia snorted loudly. "Says the one who told us that Sophia is pregnant."

"I suspected it. That's completely different."

"It's not!"

Mary's sewing machine started rattling again. "Sorry, sweetie. I can't hear you."

With that, the discussion was over, and everyone got back to work to save my wedding day.

I tried to distract myself by applying my makeup and forgetting the chaos around me, but my trembling fingers reminded me what day it was. It had to be perfect; after all, it was our wedding day!

"Say, June," Sophia began, sitting on the floor amidst pieces of fabric and sewing. "Why do you want to spend your honeymoon here instead of Paris, Dubai, or Florence?"

"Because I've been away from here for so long that I need a vacation from the world. *Red Rivers* is the most beautiful place in the world, I don't want to be anywhere else."

"I know exactly what you mean. I'm going to miss Red Rivers quite a bit, but New York just feels right."

As soon as the last harvest was in this November, Sophia would be off to New York. I already missed her, but I sincerely wished for her to find her happiness there.

Nervously, I stared at the clock, whose hands seemed to be racing.

Just in the nick of time, Mary held up the hybrid dress. It was magical, and I had to pull myself together not to burst into tears. Mary had sewn the upper part of her wedding dress to the lower part of Grandma's dress and incorporated parts of the other dress in various places. I already loved it, because I couldn't wear more of *home* than this.

"Thank you all," I sobbed. I was especially grateful to Mary, who had cut up her own wedding dress for me without batting an eye.

"Now, get in," Mary ordered with a smile.

No sooner said than done. Elli and Sophia helped me into the dress. This time, there was enough room for me and the little button.

Finally, Elli put the veil on me, and Sophia handed me the bridal bouquet.

"You look beautiful," Elli gushed.

"Like a real princess from a fairy tale!"

"A fairy tale with a *happy ending*," I said, smiling.

Lastly, Sophia and Elli put on their dresses - they were elegant, lilac-colored, and matched perfectly with my wedding dress.

We all wore our favorite boots - wedding or not, a real cowgirl doesn't wear heels, but boots!

I had thought that putting on the wedding dress would be the hardest part, but I was wrong. Only with combined efforts and a lot of patience did we manage to squeeze me into the rented limousine.

Once inside, I laughed out loud, still breathing heavily. "Before I get out, let's grease the door with Vaseline."

Mary drove us directly to the hill of *Red Rivers*, where the ceremony was taking place. John and I had chosen the location together because from there we could look out over the entire ranch. And on the horizon, we could even see the vacation ranch. The hill was simply the perfect place for our perfect wedding.

With the help of Elli and Sophia, I climbed out of the limousine, while Mary went ahead to signal everyone that we had finally arrived.

The guests, who had been quietly chatting, fell silent, and the orchestra began to play.

Elli adjusted the veil and covered my face with it. "Your big moment is coming!" Elli squealed joyfully.

My hands were shaking so hard that the bridal bouquet rustled.

"Take a deep breath, June," Sophia said with a wink, then she and Elli went ahead while I waited for my cue.

A thousand thoughts raced through my head as I stepped in front of the crowd.

What if I stumbled or stepped on the train? What if I embarrassed myself? Or worse, what if I walked down the aisle, but John wasn't there...

All my fears vanished when I took the first step forward and saw John at the end of the carpet, looking at me with pride.

My goodness, his gaze nearly knocked me out of my boots! There was a faint shimmer in his hazel eyes that grew stronger with each step I took.

I could hardly take my eyes off the man who made my heart race. He was wearing a suit but couldn't do without his cowboy hat any more than I could do without my boots. John looked perfect.

Step by step, I approached the erected arch, letting my gaze sweep over the guests. Our families, all our friends, and half of Merryville were here to celebrate with us.

Mom and Dad, both sitting in the front row, gave me proud looks, not just because I was marrying John today, but also because I had held onto my dreams and turned my grandparents' property into what we had all wished for it - a home.

When I reached John, he lifted the veil that covered my face.

"You look beautiful," he whispered in awe, and my knees went weak.

The preacher gave a short but romantic speech, just as we had wished, and then it was time for the vows.

Full of pride, John looked at me while holding my trembling hand.

"June Farley, you were the first woman I fell in love with and will always be the only one I will love."

You're wrong, John.

I had to bite my lip to keep from correcting him. There was another female being he would love just as much as me - our daughter.

Without noticing any of my thoughts, John continued with his vows.

"With you, I can laugh and cry. You are my friend, my wife, my conscience, and my heart. I will follow you anywhere, as long as my legs can carry me. I love you."

Because his words were so wonderful, I had to fight back tears.

My bridesmaids smiled at me reassuringly and silently mouthed *Breathe!*

I took a deep breath, then began my vows, which I had been pondering for weeks.

"John Key, you've been the love of my life since you stole my heart the day we first met. My heart belongs to you because I know you'll take good care of it."

I had to pause briefly. All these years, my heart had remained at *Red Rivers*, and now that I was finally here, nothing could keep me from staying.

"No matter where we are, my heart is at home with you. I love you with all my heart."

Our guests acknowledged my gesture with soft sighs.

I leaned towards John and said in a low voice, "And I'll only run as fast as your legs can carry you."

We grinned at each other, and I heard quiet giggles behind us.

Now only two things were missing: our rings and the all-important kiss.

John took my wedding ring in his hand, which sparkled beautifully in the sunlight, and took my hand.

Oh God!

Reflexively, I pulled my hand back for a moment.

My dress hadn't fit anymore, what if the ring was now too small as well?

John eyed me skeptically, but before he could ask what was going on in my head, I extended my hand to him again.

"There was a fly," I lied, grinning.

Please, please, please still fit!

I exhaled deeply, as if that could shrink my fingers.

"June Farley, will you be my wife?"

"I do," I said. God, I loved it when John looked at me like he did in that moment. So full of joy that he got little wrinkles around his eyes. Then I let John slip the ring on. I squealed with delight as I felt the ring slide over my finger and still fit perfectly.

With my newfound euphoria, I could hardly wait to take John's ring.

"John Key, will you be my husband?"

"I do," he answered in a husky voice that sent a pleasant shiver down my spine.

We were just one kiss away from being *husband and wife*, which I eagerly anticipated.

Excitedly, we both waited for the famous line. "You may now kiss the bride."

John wasted no time, grabbed me by the shoulders, pressed his lips to mine, and almost knocked me over.

It was the perfect first kiss as a married couple, and I vowed never to forget the tingling feeling in my body.

"We're married," I sobbed joyfully as we parted.

"Now you can't run away from me anymore," John murmured, grinning.

"Because there's no reason to anymore," I replied.

We turned to face our guests, who had stood up and were applauding. Almost everyone had tears in their eyes, which triggered another hormonal surge in me. At least they were euphoric tears that I was crying.

Hand in hand, John and I walked down the aisle, and for the first time, I could focus on the beautiful decorations that Sophia had set up. The white covers on the chairs had lilac-colored ribbons on the sides, which perfectly matched the bouquets of white roses and lilacs. The archway under which we had exchanged our vows was also adorned with white roses, lilacs, ribbons, and pearls.

At the end of the gathering, a carriage was waiting for us, which Sophia must have organized behind my back; I had known nothing about it.

On our way to the carriage, we accepted congratulations and hugs, especially from proud parents and grandparents.

Sophia and Elli squeezed past the crowd to greet us in front of the carriage.

"The carriage wasn't on my list," I said, grinning at Sophia.

"This is our wedding gift to you," said Sophia, linking arms with Elli.

"Yep! Packing you into a car is something none of us want to do a second time."

We giggled, then John helped me onto the fairy tale carriage, which was also decorated with purple ribbons and pulled by two large black horses that were impatiently pawing the ground.

"The carriage is perfect," I gushed without exaggeration.

"We'll take you to the holiday ranch later with this, too. The drive to *Red Rivers* is hardly worth it," said Elli and gave the coachman a signal to start.

As John and I rode to Red Rivers in the horse-drawn carriage, our guests followed us in their own cars.

"Mr. Key?" I asked.

"Yes, Mrs. Key?"

I loved how he called me Mrs. Key!

"We're married," I said in disbelief.

"Yes. Now everyone knows you belong only to me."

His voice was husky and deep, and my entire lower body clenched in anticipation.

"I can't wait for you to show me that I belong only to you," I whispered.

"Damn, me neither. Maybe we'll just leave the celebrations a bit earlier."

"But this is our wedding, John! We can't just disappear like that."

"Yes, precisely because it's our wedding, we're the only ones who have the right to leave the celebrations early," John said seriously, and I giggled.

"Okay, you're right."

"I always am."

"No," I answered, feeling argumentative. John raised an eyebrow and gave me exactly the look I had hoped for.

"We'll continue this discussion tonight," he said with a threatening voice.

"I'll remind you," I answered, winking.

Since we were leading the small convoy, we were the first to arrive at the farm.

Sophia had prepared everything here as well. On a table directly in front of the horse stable stood cakes, pies, cookies, and a thousand tons of other sweet pastries, while a huge, long table stretching across the yard was set with beautiful dishes and bouquets. The only cake on the set table was a four-tiered wedding cake.

I wondered how Sophia had managed to prepare the yard, the ceremony, and me in such a short time without going insane.

The closer we got, the more details I noticed. Even the fences and the barn were decorated with lilacs and beautiful ribbons.

Everything was so peaceful that I wished this day would never end. Champ was grazing with the other horses in the pasture behind the paddock and pricked up his ears curiously as we approached in the carriage.

I took a deep breath and enjoyed the scent of lilacs, hay, and summer.

As we came to a stop right in the yard, John got out first while I began to arrange my dress.

"May I help you out of the carriage, Mrs. Key?" he asked, extending his hand.

"I'd be delighted, Mr. Key," I replied, taking his hand.

Elli, who had been in one of the front wagons, came running towards me, squealing.

"You know what I just realized, June?"

"What's that?"

"You're a Key!"

"John might have mentioned it once or twice on the way here," I answered, smiling.

"Very good. Now you need to cut the cake so Grams can take a photo of you."

"You're hungry, aren't you?" John asked with a half-serious look.

"What makes you think that?" Elli asked innocently. But her rumbling stomach was unmistakable. "Okay, okay. Yes! I've been starving ever since Sophia forced me to help set up the buffet."

I took John's hand. "Then we should quickly make sure there's cake for everyone. We don't want to be bad hosts, do we?"

"Come on, John," Elli teased. "Be a good host."

"Behave, Elli. Or I might *accidentally* drop your favorite caramel cake," John threatened calmly.

Elli's eyes grew huge. "You wouldn't dare!"

"Want to test me?" John asked.

I knew that tone and could already hear the caramel cake hitting the ground if Elli didn't give in.

Snorting, she gave up. "Okay. I'll start handing out the champagne. How about you two?"

"Sounds good," said John, while I simultaneously yelled "No!"

Startled by my own volume, I moderated myself. "I mean, maybe later. But we shouldn't get drunk in the middle of the day."

"Yes, you're absolutely right, June! I'll bring you some juice," Elli said with wide eyes.

"What are you two up to?" John asked, his gaze shifting between me and Elli.

"Absolutely nothing," I said innocently.

"We'll talk about this tonight," John muttered.

I nodded uncertainly. Then we turned back to our guests. More and more guests were arriving at the yard, mingling in small groups and chatting.

As I let my gaze wander across the yard, I saw Sophia tending to the horses along with the coachman.

"Excuse me for a moment," I said to John, his grandma, and my parents, then walked over to Sophia.

"You look happy," Sophia said joyfully.

"I'm the happiest bride in the world, and I owe a large part of that to you," I said and hugged Sophia. "Thank you for arranging everything so perfectly."

"Oh, June, I was happy to do it," Sophia replied, touched. "You wanted a perfect wedding, and you deserved it."

I smiled gratefully at Sophia. She was truly too good for this world!

"We're about to cut the cake. I thought I'd let you know so you can grab a piece before the buffet battle begins."

"That's sweet of you! I'll just quickly take these two horses to the pasture, then I'll come."

The coachman was taking care of the leather harnesses while Sophia led the black horses to the pasture to rest before continuing on to the holiday ranch.

Just as I was about to go back to John, it happened. The tail of the black horse on Sophia's left got tangled with the tablecloth of the large table. With a powerful swish of its tail, the horse tried to free itself, but what had to happen, happened. The jerk caused glasses and plates to crash to the ground with a clatter, spooking both horses. Sophia had no chance against the colossi, which both ran across the yard while the entire place setting fell to the ground with a clinking sound.

Murmurs and whispers broke out among the guests as I rushed to Sophia, who was staring at the chaos right in front of her with an open mouth and wide eyes.

"Oh God," she sighed.

"Are you okay?" I asked.

Sophia was on the verge of tears. "I've ruined your wedding."

By now, the coachman had his horses under control again. The troublemaker, whose tail was still tangled with the tablecloth, was distracted by the four-tiered - completely smashed - cake, which he was licking off the ground with relish.

John, who had also rushed to help his sister, grabbed her chin and turned her head.

"Sophia, are you alright?" he asked a second time.

She shook her head. "No! I've ruined your wedding. This chaos is even worse than at the barbecue back then!"

While Sophia stood crying in front of me and the guests stared in dismay at the pile of shards, I burst into raucous laughter. But this time it wasn't because the little button inside me was messing with my hormones, but because it was simply funny.

I took Sophia in my arms. "I wanted the perfect wedding. And I wanted the wedding to be talked about forever. Thanks to you, both have come true."

No one had forgotten Sophia's barbecue incident yet, and that was long ago. The chances were really good that my wedding would be forever etched in Merryville's gossip.

Sophia looked at me questioningly. "You're not mad at me?"

"No, of course not."

Sophia sighed. "But your wedding cake."

"The horses can have it, it's not a big deal. There are plenty of other cakes."

I still hadn't convinced Sophia, as she now stared glumly at the broken porcelain. "All the dishes are broken. What will everyone eat on?"

I looked around for Mary. If anyone had an idea, it would be her. "Your Grams will sort it out. And now stop crying, for goodness' sake, you'll set me off!"

Bravely, Sophia wiped away her tears, and before I could even ask Mary, she had already found a solution. She distributed paper plates to all the guests, while John's brothers cleared away the mess in no time.

And what can I say? The cakes tasted excellent on plates featuring the *Avengers*, the *Justice League*, and *My Little Pony*.

Everything was exactly as I had wished for. It was perfect and would be memorable for everyone, which would never have happened without the carriage horse's unintentional stunt performance.

Right on time for sunset, the coachman took us to our honeymoon, which we spent in the most beautiful place in the world - home.

The holiday ranch was just as beautifully decorated, and John's string lights made everything glow brightly. He helped me out of the carriage and led me to the entrance of our small, sweet home.

"Ready for your wedding night, Mrs. Key?" he asked with a smile. His eyes gleamed darkly, and I could hardly wait to finally be alone with him.

"Ready, Mr. Key," I replied, and John grabbed me, lifted me up, and carried me directly over the threshold, as a true gentleman should.

We were home, and although I knew we weren't living in a fairy tale, I was certain that we would be happy until the end of our days, because after all the escapes, goodbyes, and reunions, we had more than earned our happy ending.

Epilogue – John

FINALLY, I COULD CARRY my wife over the threshold of our home. I had waited all day for this, if not my entire life. June was undoubtedly the most beautiful bride in the world, and I could hardly believe she was mine.

As I crossed the threshold, her sweet scent enveloped me, which I deeply inhaled. I wanted this scent to be the first thing I noticed upon waking and the last before sleeping. "Welcome home," I said and gently set June down.

"Finally," she replied, smiling.

The path had been rocky, but we hadn't given up, and so we were rewarded.

June looked beautiful in her wedding dress, yet I could hardly wait to see her naked again.

June shyly looked down, knowing as well as I did what awaited us on our wedding night. I raised her chin and made her look at me.

"I love you," I whispered.

"I love you too," June whispered back, smiling.

We kissed, first slowly and sensually, then increasingly urgently. I couldn't get enough of her soft lips and licked her lower lip until she willingly opened her mouth for my tongue to enter. Our tongues greeted each other fiercely. June's gasps grew louder, making the space in my pants unbearably tight.

Breathlessly, we broke apart. I turned June around and opened her corset.

"John?" June asked.

"What is it?"

"I have something for you."

Her voice was soft and trembled slightly, just as it often did when I introduced new, exciting things to her. Of course, I had something very special prepared for her today.

"That can wait. First, I'll make sure you have an unforgettable wedding night," I said and freed June from the corset.

"But..."

A single glance silenced her.

"Later," I said in a gruff voice and kissed her neck. "First, I want to give you memories."

Memories and a few leather items I had acquired. My wife hesitated, then nodded. Together, we removed the rest of her dress until she stood naked before me.

I licked over her nipples, which stiffened and reached out to me. My fingers stroked her soft, flawless skin, rewarded by June's moan.

"Kneel before me on the floor!" I commanded gently.

June obeyed immediately.

"Good girl," I praised her. Then I lit the candles I had placed on the dressers and nightstands. I turned off all other light sources. Only the warm candlelight enveloped us.

From the large wardrobe, I took out my gifts for June. Just the thought of how she would wear the leather restraints made things even tighter in my pants.

Of course, I could have undressed, but I loved the contrast my clothes created between us. She, completely naked and submissive, while I exuded pure dominance.

"Stretch your wrists forward!" I demanded.

June's eyes lit up, and I rewarded her with a smile. She enjoyed our games as much as I did, even though we played by my rules—and today, I would introduce new rules.

I put the first leather restraint on June, which gently molded to her skin. There were eyelets on the sides, which I could connect with chains or ropes. After I had put on the second restraint, I kissed her wrists and deeply inhaled the scent she exuded.

Lilac and leather, a great combination.

Finally, I put a leather collar around her neck. I enjoyed the sight before me. "You look beautiful," I whispered. June smiled up at me.

The humility suited June well, and the leather restraints made her shine.

"Spread your legs a bit wider and place your hands, palms up, on them!" I commanded.

June immediately followed my order and spread her legs wide enough for my hand to slide between them.

I groaned as I felt her wetness.

"Believe me, baby. I can hardly wait to fuck you."

"Then take me."

My fingers rubbed June's pearl while she moved her hips in rhythm.

"You'll have to wait a little longer."

June looked at me, tormented. She didn't want to wait any longer; she wanted to feel my hard cock inside her, but precisely for that reason, she had to be patient a little longer. I simply loved playing with her desire and driving her to the brink of madness until she almost lost her mind. There were no more intense orgasms for both of us, because the waiting made me at least as hungry as June.

I took a delicate chain, fastened it first to June's left wrist, then pulled it through the ring around her neck before attaching it to her other wrist as well.

Then I stood two steps away from her, admiring my work.

Damn, just the sight of it almost made me come. June on her knees, in perfect submissive posture, with a hungry gaze. The leather cuffs suited her perfectly, and I already knew they would see frequent use.

"Tonight, I will make you scream with lust and pain," I said.

June bit her lip. I could see she could hardly wait for the release.

"You might scream things you don't really mean, so we need a safeword," I continued. "You know what a safeword is?"

June nodded. "Kryptonite."

"Kryptonite," I repeated. I liked her safeword.

"Yes."

"Good girl," I said. "You've earned a reward for that."

My hard cock practically sprang out of my open pants. June eagerly opened her mouth, ready for me to thrust it deep into her.

Wrong thought, baby.

I only stepped close enough for the tip to touch her lips. June leaned forward a bit, and I leaned back just as far.

Sighing, she stuck out her tongue and licked my glans while looking at me with pleading eyes.

"Do you want more?" I asked, and June nodded.

I pushed my cock a little further into her mouth and allowed her to suck on it. Her lips wrapped tightly around me as her tongue continued to lick in circular motions.

Breathing heavily, I leaned my head back and enjoyed June's tongue.

Only when I could no longer hold back did I thrust deeper into her throat.

Fuck. So warm. So wet. So damn tight!

I repeatedly thrust my hard erection into her mouth, watching June with wide, glowing eyes. Her lips closed tightly around my erection, urging me to my peak. When June then started to suck, I let go of all restraint. I buried my hands in her hair and thrust to the hilt.

June's entire body trembled with desire, her eyes screamed for more, and I was determined to fulfill her wish. She got more of it, harder and deeper.

It felt good to be inside her, so good that I wasted no time and took June until I poured myself into her, pumping.

June licked her lips and swallowed my seed with a smile.

"Now it's your turn," I whispered, as my cock still stood ready to fuck June a second time.

Smiling contentedly, June wanted to get up, but I stopped her.

"Stay, I love it when you kneel in front of me!"

There was no need for June to stand up. I hadn't just bought leather cuffs in town, but also a vibrator that was astonishingly powerful.

June eyed the long rod, whose rounded tip vibrated, and groaned loudly as I pushed it between her legs.

"Oh God!" she groaned.

I watched with fascination as her breasts swayed with each breath. June really had perfect breasts, full and round, and I imagined rubbing my cock between them.

Her entire body screamed for an orgasm, and I was determined to allow it.

"Do you want to come?" I asked.

"Yes, definitely!"

"You may - but first, you have to endure a few more clamps for me."

I set the vibrator aside so my good girl would stay good and not come without my permission.

"No!" June ordered me. I paused. Had June really just yelled at me? Was she so close to orgasm, or did it have something to do with the clamps I wanted to get?

"No?" My look signaled to her that she should think carefully about her next answer.

"Please, no clamps," June panted.

No clamps? Ever since June had first experienced the pleasure of clamps, she had been insatiable for them. Although... in the past few weeks, June had been downright decent.

"What would you like me to endure instead?" I asked.

"How about some strikes?" I nodded, but June wasn't done. "On the soles of the feet."

I raised an eyebrow questioningly, and June responded with a determined look.

Strikes on the soles of the feet caused pain on a whole different level than clamps. June had never endured such strikes before, but I was a gentleman and obliged her wish.

I opened the cabinet and let my fingers glide over various whips and sticks. I paused briefly at the bamboo cane, but for a warm-up, a softer whip was better.

"So, you want to scream for me tonight," I stated.

"Yes," June replied resolutely.

"Good."

I unchained her from her restraints and June sighed as she let her arms fall. But I didn't give her time to catch her breath, as I quickly bound her hands behind her back again.

I slipped my arm under hers, helping her up and leading her to the table at the other end of the room, where I bent her over it. June looked irresistible, her ass high in the air, waiting for me to finally fuck her.

Not yet, darling.

My hand slipped between her legs, and I pushed two fingers inside her, giving her a taste of what was to come if she endured everything. Then I indulged myself in her sweet pleasure by licking my fingers clean.

I had paid too little attention to June's legs, but I made up for it now. To ensure June stayed where I wanted her, I played it safe and fastened two more leather cuffs to her ankles, securing them to the table legs. Now, no matter what June wanted to do, she would stay in place.

"I like it when you surrender to me like this," I said in a husky voice.

Then I stroked her back, ass, and thighs with the flogger, whose end was equipped with a wide leather strip.

When I reached the inside of her thighs, the caresses turned into real strikes.

The leather cracked louder on her skin, just like her moans.

You're still moaning, my beauty. Soon you'll be screaming for me.

I intensified the strength of my strikes until I was sure June would still feel my treatment tomorrow when she sat in the saddle. Then I turned my attention to her well-shaped calves. This time, it wasn't the leather tip that hit her skin, but the leather-wrapped rod, which was more painful than the small leather paddle at the tip.

June groaned loudly as she futilely tried to free herself from her restraints. The next strike followed, and June arched her back again.

To further emphasize June's helplessness, I pressed her upper body harder onto the table with my left hand while continuing to work on her calves.

Her groans quickly turned into soft pleading, followed by loud pleading. I admired her endurance, for no matter how hard my strikes were, June bit her lips together and endured the pain without even thinking of our safeword.

Even when the whip hit the same spot multiple times in a row, bringing tears to June's eyes, she didn't say a word.

My brave, courageous girl.

As my strikes grew harder, it became wetter between June's legs.

"Ready for the soles of the feet?" I asked with a smile, and June nodded.

I swapped the flogger for a bamboo cane, then released the left ankle cuff and stretched her foot toward her ass.

Although my first strike was very restrained, June flinched and tried to pull her foot away from me. But she had no chance against my firm grip.

"The more strikes you can endure now, the more intense your orgasm will be." I said calmly. June reflexively tried to pull her foot away again and again, but the protest stopped as soon as I punished her with harder strikes.

"Do you want to be fucked now?"

Yes, it was mean to strike only one spot, to strike harder with each blow and to let less time pass between the strikes, but June had wanted it this way.

My strikes brought tears to her eyes, but she bravely endured until I released her foot, reattached it to the table, and turned my attention to the other foot. There, the game began anew. This time, June was smart enough not to evade me again, to avoid further strikes.

Upon reaching the end of the procedure, I also reattached her second leg to the table.

"Do you want to be fucked by me now?" I asked.

"Yes, please!" June begged me. She willingly offered her ass to me, and I fulfilled her wish.

I rubbed my hard erection against her wet entrance, then thrust deeply, eliciting a blissful moan from June.

Her tight walls massaged me so well that I was on the brink of coming a second time. But this time, I let June take the lead; she had more than earned her orgasm.

"Come for me," I whispered.

I knew June's preferences inside and out, so I knew exactly that I had to fuck her hard to make her come within a few minutes.

June's skin glistened, and her sensual moan echoed through the warm air. I loved it when she looked at me with such love, as she did right now. That was the look men like me longed for; I needed those looks like air to breathe.

Just before June came, she tightened around me, and I gripped her hips firmly to thrust even harder. Her entire body tensed, then relaxed, and the saving orgasm washed away the madness I had caused in her.

Breathless, June let herself fall back onto the table, and her tightness forced me to orgasm as well.

For a moment, I rested my head on June's back to catch my breath. I inhaled her sweet scent that had settled on her salty skin.

"That was..." June began, but then faltered, lacking the right words. I knew exactly what she meant. It had been perfect, and it wasn't over yet.

"That was just the beginning," I replied. My voice sounded rough and dark.

"What?" June asked, shocked.

"I promised you that you'd scream all night," I answered. "You know I keep my promises."

June looked at me with wide eyes. "I need a break."

Although I would have loved to fuck June right away, I released her restraints and carried her to our marital bed. She was still breathing heavily, and her cool skin was covered in sweat.

Her eyelids fluttered, half from exhaustion, half from the fading orgasm. Until her breathing calmed down, I stroked her soft skin. We still had the whole night ahead of us, and the night after that, and the night after that. We had all the time in the world, so I was willing to give June enough time to recover.

"Tell me, June. Why the soles of the feet?" I asked, thoughtfully pushing a brown strand from her face.

"It's complicated," June sighed.

"Explain it to me anyway."

"I didn't want you to accidentally hit my belly or for the clamps to cause damage there."

I furrowed my brow. "Has that ever happened?"

My heart suddenly pounded so loudly that it echoed in my temples. June shook her head. "No, but still."

"Why are you suddenly worrying about that?"

"Because I have to worry about it."

What the hell? What was June talking about? My first thought was that she had drunk too much at our wedding, but that was out of the question since June hadn't touched a single drop of alcohol.

"Do I need to worry too?" I asked.

"Yes," June replied seriously.

Damn, what was going on?

Breathlessly, June turned to the side, opened the drawer of her nightstand, and pulled out a small velvet bag, which she pressed into my hand.

"Open it, and you'll understand."

I felt the black, soft bag, which didn't contain much. When I opened it, I pulled out a black-and-white image—an ultrasound.

Was June sick? The thought that June might have a serious illness made me feel sick. But I wasn't a doctor and had no idea what I was supposed to see in the image.

When she saw my gaze, she whispered, "There's something else in the bag."

June was right; there was something hard and elongated in the bag that I pulled out.

My gaze flicked back and forth between her and the pregnancy test. "Really?"

"Really."

Now I realized what the small bubble on the image was—my child, our child!

In disbelief and full of awe, I stroked June's flat belly. Did the tiny bubble even have enough room in there?

"You need to eat more," I said thoughtfully, and June giggled.

"If you knew how often I've raided your sisters' ice cream stash, you'd say something different." Then her expression grew serious again. "Are you happy?"

My eyes filled with tears. That was answer enough, as I rarely showed such emotion.

"Damn, I'm the happiest man on the whole planet."

I hugged June, who was also close to tears, and suddenly I understood what had been going on with her in the last few weeks. All her mood swings, which I had attributed to the upcoming wedding, had actually been a sign of our impending happiness.

With eagle eyes, I searched the ultrasound image for my child, but I couldn't find it.

June took the image from me with a smile and pointed to a tiny, black dot.

"That's our button," she gushed.

"Now I see him," I replied with a smile.

Crazy. What was on the image was really my child. I still couldn't believe it.

"Him? I think it's going to be a girl," she corrected me.

"No." I leaned my head right up against June's belly. "You're going to be a strapping cowboy with broad shoulders, just like your dad."

"Or it's going to be a cowgirl who shows the Key boys what girl power means," June replied, winking. "I guess we'll just have to be surprised."

Whether it was a boy or a girl, I already knew that I wanted more children, because the feeling of becoming a father was incredible!

"I promise you that this blind date in a few months will be just as perfect as our wedding day."

"It will be," June replied, rubbing her belly.

Could my life get any better? No, damn it. I was the happiest man on the planet.

We lay there for a long time, just stroking June's belly, where a strapping cowboy—I knew it would be a boy—was growing.

"Should I make you scream again?" I asked, grinning.

"Are you serious, John?"

"Should I not?" June could claim whatever she wanted, but I knew exactly that she was insatiable and longed for me to confront her again with lust, pain, and all the gray areas in between.

June bit her lower lip thoughtfully. "Okay, caught."

"Then tell me what I should do with you next," I whispered.

I'll do anything you want with you, all night long.

Every single night. Forever.

If you would like to receive a free novel and be alerted when my next book is published, visit: https://lana-stone.com/. There, like over 9000 fans before you, you can sign up for my newsletter.

Printed in Great Britain
by Amazon